THE DEADLY
DOVE

THE DEADLY DOVE

RUFUS KING

WILDSIDE PRESS

CHAPTER I

Two events set the stage.

They occurred in September: the month, appropriately enough, of storms. Their points of origin were one racketeer (emeritus, with honorable discharge from the Volstead era) and one wealthy old museum piece with the stellar-eyed outlook on life of a diligent cobra.

New York was not at its best. The weather was foul.

At nine o'clock in the morning Joe Inbrun got up. The windows of his bedroom looked east, high above Central Park, and the sky was as dreary as a sick tomato. This was the same penthouse in which Joe had lived since his racketeer activities during prohibition.

Although currently a thrifty and substantial citizen of means, with a lucrative penchant for backing night clubs and plays, Joe's ethics were unchanged: an eye for an eye.

Joe slipped neat feet into slippers and put on a dressing gown over his pajamas, adding outrage to outrage. He walked into a garish living room and rang for Felix.

Felix came in with the morning paper. Felix was a furtive, saddened individual who had been Joe's general servant since the penthouse had been leased. His clothes and manner were strictly *de rigueur* with the best upper-bracket-mob interpretation of an English butler. Felix would never leave Joe because he knew that if he ever attempted to Joe would see to it that he fried.

They mutually agreed that the morning stank, and Joe sat down to look at the news while Felix returned to the kitchen and got busy about breakfast. This always was a hearty one, and Felix rarely failed to pale and tremble visibly as the daily urge obsessed him to add a dash of *sauce arsenic* to the coddled eggs.

A picture on page three of the newspaper held Joe. Its caption read:

The picture was of a handsome, muscular youth with large Irish eyes and dark wavy hair. The woman clinging to the young man's arm looked definitely maternal, if not downright grandmotherly, in & startlingly smart way.

Under the picture it said:

> Alan Jefferson Admont and the former Mrs. Christine Belder at Nativity Church, Kingston, N. Y., yesterday.

Joe said he would be damned.

He read the item. It was a neat job, a hairline this side of slander. The wedding rated news value, rather than mere space among the social notes, because of Christine Belder.

Christine was, the item said, the widow of Charles Belder, research engineer and capitalist. Most of her married life had been spent with her husband abroad, where her somewhat eccentric divertissements among the international set had been a caution.

Following Belder's death three years ago, Christine had retired to their mountain fastness, Belder Tor, at Dour Notch in the Catskills; an estate which embraced a peak whose elevation almost rivaled that of Roundtop and whose virginal loneliness far surpassed it. Christine's age (she made no bones about it) was sixty.

The item then started in on Alan, and the going got rough. Although only twenty-five, the draft had rejected him. Period. It then inferred that a well-kept career had carried Alan through several seasons of being a juvenile lead with summer and lesser stock companies. It lingered on Alan's having hit Broadway last year for a rubber-curtain run in a play and production of his own: *Jupiter Returns*. He had managed, it was said, to induce Joe Inbrun to back this turkey to the extent, it was said, of twenty-five thousand dollars.

The item did not fail to indicate that Joe Inbrun, currently a Broadway angel and an ex-character of a genus less seraphic, must have been suffering some sort of mental aberration ever to have been roped in as such a sucker.

Joe took time out from reading to bite viciously the end from a cigar.

The article said the show had been unique in that *Variety* had given *Jupiter Returns*, the shortest notice of the season: Jupe Didn't. But the performance had brought Alan's facade to Christine's attention inasmuch as she had attended the opening night. Her quote on this was: "My heart bled at the way both the audience and the critics pilloried that sterling artist."

A mutual friend had taken Christine backstage and had introduced her, and she had persuaded Alan to renounce an art whose victories, for him, would at their best be Pyrrhic and to accept the post of her social secretary. That had been a year ago. And now they were wed.

Christine's final quote was: "There will be no honeymoon. With transportation at a premium and with every non-essential expense a sabotaging of the war effort, my husband and I will continue our quiet and simple manner of living at Belder Tor for the duration. Afterward, of course, who knows?"

Joe thoughtfully lighted the savagely bitten cigar.

Among his attributes was a large sense of pride encased in a very thin skin. He never forgot a debt or a slur. Nor did he ever forgive. Even though a year had passed, his fiasco and monetary loss via Alan still held their full measure of bitter gall.

He went to a telephone and put in a person-to-person call for Mr. Alan Jefferson Admont, Belder Tor, Dour Notch, the Catskills. He looked acidly at Felix who came in, not with breakfast, but with Belle Crystal.

Belle was getting on, but as little as she and every expensive aid could help it. Once a week her figure was rolled back to slenderness at a pretty cost. Her furs and style were elegant. She could still do the split.

She went to Joe and kissed him, through an accompanying cloud of Genet's Sauve-qui-peut, while her big, hard blue eyes flickered restlessly about the room.

Joe looked at her stonily.

"Get hailed out?" he asked.

"Silly!"

She could tell that he was anything but pleased at seeing her and that he was wondering what had made her drop in like this in the morning. Beneath her carefully tended beauty (luscious type) Belle was a thoroughly selfish and conniving woman as well as a conceited one. Her previous-to-Joe-benefactor had hit the nail squarely when he had called her a Baked Alaska flavored with essence of Asp.

Her flickered survey assured Belle the living room offered no traces other than the purely masculine. For some time she had been increasingly suspicious about the tensile strength of her hold on Joe. She had decided on making this early sortie to give the familiar arena an unexpected once-over.

Fully aware of the tactical values of demand-and-attack, Belle turned on a modicum of sex and said: "It's about a little jacket I saw in Saks as I was walking uptown, Joe."

"Buy it."

She kissed him again. She said that he was sweet. She said that the jacket was chinchilla. The phone rang.

"Al?" Joe said into it. "Joe."

Alan's voice usually held a warm, hypnotic quality which had served his young and not uneventful life very well. At the moment it was tempered with a faint chill. He was disturbed and considerably puzzled that Joe should call him up, and he detested being called Al.

He had never been quite happy about Joe. He knew the usual stories: how several of Joe's friends had suddenly and inexplicably vanished from the passing scene, nor was anyone ever so gauche as to inquire where they went.

"Hello there, Joe." Alan did his best to sound cordial. His tones swung into their British register. Nothing pleased Alan better than to have a person say: You talk just like an Englishman. "I suppose you want to congratulate me and all of that, what?"

"I will tell you what I want when I see you. I will be out."

There was a slender pause during which Alan's British accent did a backslide toward the Middle West.

"I'll run in, Joe. I'll go into town to see you. It will be like old times."

"No."

"Not that I wouldn't be tickled to death to have you out here, but you know how it is." Alan gave his best deprecatory little laugh. It had always gone over like hot cakes with the matinee houses. "Christine isn't going in much for entertaining right now."

Joe repeated flatly: "I am coming out."

"Look, then—could you make it this morning? Christine is driving into town. Can you make it about eleven?"

"I'll be there at eleven."

Joe hung up.

"Was that Al Admont?" Belle asked.

"Yes."

Belle was deeply interested. She had gone through Joe's purchase of Alan's goose egg and had tempered Joe's steaming morale during the blistering he had been handed by the press. Although an exceedingly cold baby in her own right, Belle had felt colder still at the way Joe had been cold when he had read the early editions' plastering of *Jupiter Returns*. She had felt her strongest chill when Joe had given Alan a ring and had said: "It's all right, Al. I'll fix it up later."

The remark hadn't made much sense until Belle had thought it over. Joe was bursting with health today because of that principle of his of always letting a lot of time elapse between cause and effect. Joe had once said to her about this: "It bewilders the motive."

She had more than a shrewd suspicion that the present telephone call indicated that the time had come for Joe to collect the year-old loss on *Jupiter Returns* from Alan, via Alan's just-acquired rich wife. Belle's greedy, conniving, moderate mind glowed tentatively with dangerous fires. The band wagon, in the sense of the Belder fortune, was a roomy one. Might there not, she asked herself, be a seat aboard it for her too?

"I read about the wedding," she said. "Al certainly landed on his feet. On all four of them."

"Go get that jacket, Belle," Joe said.

CHAPTER II

Joe headed his convertible toward the Catskills. The car was a stunning job in lemon yellow with white-walled black-market tires, but Joe missed the old bullet-proof bus. He still, even after many years of secure tranquility, felt like a soft-shelled crab without its armor.

Belder Tor, when Joe reached it, was impressive, in the dolorous and chilling fashion that a Rhineland castle can be impressive. Its mass was granite gray against the large estate's uninhabited reaches of forested hilltops, while the distant peak of Roundtop offered a grim background against a glimmer and sullen sky. No sound broke the stillness. Not even a bird flashed past on slanting wing. Definitely one hell of a place to live.

Joe parked the car and sat thoughtfully casing the layout. He supposed some local hunter or fisherman might drift past once in a blue moon, but otherwise what? He got out of the car as he saw Alan open the front door and walk down shallow granite steps.

Alan, in person, was even handsomer than his picture, and his physique was closer to a light heavyweight's than to that of an actor. His costume, in several shades of taupe, was carelessly Pinehurst. A large star sapphire in tortured gold accented a smoothly tanned finger. It was a curious ring in that two golden lion paws held the stone in place with delicate claws of platinum. He had admired it greatly, and Christine (with a shudder) had bought it for him.

He had been drinking steadily since Joe had telephoned, in a nervous effort to bolster his courage against he knew not what. The liquor, and Alan's ability to dramatize any situation into a mold which struck him as most comfortable, had done the trick. He felt perfectly at ease: a young baronet welcoming a tiresome guest to the family rookery with an appropriate amount of *noblesse oblige*.

"Joe, old pal!"

Alan sought and briefly held Joe's unresponsive hand, and Joe followed him into an entrance hall murky with tapestries and suits of armor. The armor bemused Joe's attention while he mentally compared it with bulletproof vests. "Let us," Alan said in clipped British-baronet tones, "get out of this set for Dracula and go into the morning room. It's the one spot in the house where you can talk and not spit out vampires."

The morning room, because of its sweep of french windows, was somewhat but not much better. Its decor leaned glumly toward further tapestries of the more morbid genre, with an occasional mounted head of the less attractive wild animals. Through the french windows and doors, which opened onto a flagged terrace, lay the view of a small mountain lake and beyond it a terrifying background of the Catskill's gloomier peaks.

The atmosphere started to oppress Joe. He was very sensitive to atmospheres, and this one held a predominant emptiness: a deserted quality. He stood at a window and watched the dark forest and the calm, sullen lake. All he could think of was Indians. "How do you run a joint like this?" he said. "Where can you get the help?"

"We can't. We do it ourselves."

"You and your wife?"

"No. Christine has three friends staying here. She is a woman who is not unversed in collecting her pound of flesh. They all pitch in. Scotch, Joe?"

"Yes."

Alan went to a cellaret and mixed drinks. He gave a highball to Joe and suggested that they sit down.

"So that's the setup. Just you and your wife and three friends." Joe sat down. He took a drink. It was important that he know who these people were. This data was equally as important as a general knowledge of the house and grounds. He asked casually: "Who are they, Al?"

Alan was both puzzled and pleased at this interest of Joe's in the Belder Tor ménage. Of course it was leading up to something, to whatever purpose (unpleasant) which had brought Joe up, but at least it retained the scene on its comforting social plane.

"They're a trio of satellites, Joe. My wife's. Shall we start with Godfrey Lance?"

Alan tossed the cue to Joe, who left it flat. That was the trouble with these heavy dimwits who were not of the profession. Nothing short of a *diseur* could hope to cope with them.

He went on: "Godfrey is a painter. Born somewhere in Brooklyn in one of those outlying regions miles away from the Heights." Alan pursed handsome lips judiciously. He felt the incipience of a mot. "I suppose you could call him a refugee-expatrie. From Paris." He indicated a painting on the west wall. The star-sapphire ring flashed handsomely with the gesture. "That's one of his things."

Joe examined the canvas in complete bewilderment. "What is it?"

"It is a portrait of Christine. Godfrey's métier lies in doing portraits of his sitters' psychoses. He had a one-man show at the Lewis Galleries last spring which had the town back on its heels. Christine went to it and picked up one of his little numbers. Portrait of a Toad. It was his only sale. She also picked up Godfrey."

"Just what is she, anyhow? A nymph?"

Alan laughed pleasantly.

"It's nothing like that. She isn't interested in that stuff at all. L'amour, for Christine, is definitely in the sere. Even if it weren't, Godfrey's around forty and has the sex appeal of a balloon. He's a damn good cook."

"Does she pay him to stay here and cook?"

"No, Christine doesn't work things that way."

Alan frowned. Even after a year with her, Christine still bewildered him: the fact that people fell for her like shot ducks, that they couldn't *see* through her the way that he did. He still retained a grudging admiration for her wit and for the prestidigitatorial perfection of her Lady Bountiful act. Or was the act more closely akin to a mischievous goddess who both confounded and adjusted the lives of other people from her machine?

He said: "I suppose what it really amounts to is that Christine dopes out her beloved dependents' little weaknesses and caters to them. They may struggle to get out of her talons, but the clutch holds firm. Godfrey's vice is food, so she stuffs him with black-market delicacies. As a result, he fiddles around every morning daubing up a canvas and cooks three meals a day. He loves it."

Joe filed Godfrey in his mental notebook. Christine was beginning to make good sense to him: she operated in much the same manner as he did in regard to Felix. "She is not such a dope at that."

"Anything but. Take Cordelia—Cordelia Banning. Her great-great-grandfather Blucher, or something, was one of the early mayors of New York."

Alan lighted a cigarette while permitting Joe to sit there and take Cordelia.

"Cordelia," he said, "is a dear, vague old thing and an incurable shoplifter. Naturally her breeding and good taste prevent her from lifting any but the best things. Say some exquisite little brooch or similar bijouterie."

Joe's opinion of Christine's good sense evaporated. "What does your wife do? Fence the stuff?"

"Scarcely." Alan gave Joe his profile and smile. "Cordelia takes care of the few rooms we use. She also does the catering, a job peculiarly fitted to her shoplifting proclivities. Primarily, of course, she amuses Christine beyond words. Every time Cordelia brings home the unbilled caviar Christine is in stitches. She caught on to Cordelia at a jeweler's and whisked her away in her car just as the clerk was beginning to wonder about a pair of teardrop earrings."

Joe was not entirely happy about Cordelia. He checked her off with mental reservations.

"Who is your third nut?" he asked.

"He is a doctor. Dr. Hugo Wintersweet. Hugo diddled with some unorthodox antics and they drummed him out of the Medical Association. There was a splash in the papers over some fatal case, and Christine hooked him. She set up a laboratory for his use in the game room, where he kids himself he can finish his experiments and be re-established."

"What does Christine get out of it?"

"Hugo is an excellent chauffeur and general mechanic, as well as having a strong sardonic streak which pleases her. I suppose she feels like a lion tamer every time Hugo brings around the car. Another scotch, Joe?"

"Yes." Joe thought the list over. "She should have run into a mess before now, picking up characters like that."

"She did. There was some trouble a couple of years ago, before this present bunch was installed."

Joe said with careful interest: "Just what happened, Al?"

"Some woman. Christine doesn't speak about it much, but we all know it worries her. This woman blew her top when Christine eased her out. Said she'd *get* Christine for discarding her like an old glove, or some such wretched cliché."

"What had Christine done to her?"

"Nothing, according to Christine. I suppose the woman felt she was set for life in the lap-of-luxury sort of thing and got steamed up over being thrown out. Just one of those messes, Joe."

"What was this woman's name? Where is she now?"

"God knows. Christine simply speaks of her as Laura. She dusts off the menacing Laura whenever she needs an example of Ingratitude to shake in our faces. Why?"

"Laura," said Joe thoughtfully, "might fit in with what I am out here for. We'll see."

"Just what does bring you out here, Joe?"

"Twenty-five thousand dollars."

So here it was. Alan drank deeply. It gave him a breathing spell to curtain his mind against the number of shocking avenues along which Joe's statement might lead. His smile emerged pleasant and fresh.

"You took a chance on *Jupiter Returns*," he said. "It was a gamble, and you lost."

"I never lose. Not even when I do."

"I don't get it, Joe."

"How much did she kick in to get you to the altar?"

"Christine? Nothing. Not a cent."

Joe studied Alan for a quiet moment.

"Better wipe that sweat off your forehead. Don't be nervous."

"I'm not."

"How much was it, Al?"

"Nothing. I told you so." Alan added sullenly: "She made a will."

"I suppose she left you the works?"

"Yes."

"Sap!"

"Why? What have I got to lose?"

Joe said patiently: "You will get what she decides to give you until she changes the will and boots you out. She will get tired of you in the same way she got tired of that Laura woman."

"Not a chance. She's hooked, Joe."

Joe went on speculatively sizing Alan up, the way he had sized up a good many people in his career to their ultimate disadvantage or worse. He wondered briefly what slip of judgment had caused him to put his chips on Alan in the first place. Subconsciously he knew it had been the youngster's very convincing line of talk and a certain charm that, even with Joe's, was all but hypnotic.

"Would your wife fix you up with a personal bank account, Al? Would she let you manage her securities?"

"No, her lawyer does that. Stuyvesant Swain. The old buzzard handles some of the biggest estates in the country. Christine's income isn't anywhere near what it was when her husband was alive, Joe. When they built this place."

"What do you think she'd cut up for?"

"Maybe not more than half a million."

"What do you get for cigarettes, Al?"

"She gives me the same as I got as her secretary."

"Scratch feed."

Alan thought this over. The alcohol and his acute powers for self-dramatization gave emphasis to the truth of Joe's gibe. He discarded the role of worldly young baronet.

"Don't I know it?" he said bitterly. "Honestly, Joe," he added, the ham in him breaking out, "do you know what I feel like sometimes? It's—well, it's like being a golden falcon caged into lifelong servitude through the machinations of a rich old witch."

Joe let this pass.

"About this will—have you seen it, or did she just tell you about it?"

"She showed it to me. It's why she decided to marry me. She wanted to leave me her money but was afraid that a porcupine grandniece who's her ward would contest the will unless I was her husband."

Joe thought the grandniece over. It never paid, he had discovered, to overlook the smallest detail of a picture. "Does this grandniece hang around?"

"No. Her name's Lida Belder, and Christine keeps her in the best girls' schools and ships her off for vacations with her school friends. I've never seen her. Christine has an allergy to the callow young. In skirts."

"Orphan?"

"Yes. Her parents blew up on a yacht or something."

"Where is she now?"

"Visiting some people called Vanbuskirk up at Bar Harbor, I believe."

Joe finished his drink and put the glass down.

"Did I ever tell you about the Dove?" he asked.

"No."

"He was one of my guns back in the old days."

A strange excitement raced through Alan. Being fundamentally amoral about everything, he certainly was so about this tentative implication concerning Christine's welfare.

"What about him, Joe?"

"The Dove is still one of my guns."

Alcohol fumed further, and Christine was crystal sharp in Alan's mind. Heaven knew that often enough he had speculated as to how long a stretch it would be before she kicked off and left him holding the golden bag.

He found himself blurting out tensely: "Murder isn't safe, Joe."

"It's all according."

Alan looked at him in fascination. He took in Joe's calm, well-massaged face, the noncommittal eyes.

"I suppose you could even get used to it?"

"I will tell you more," Joe said, "about the Dove. He is a gentlemanly, mild-mannered old guy, and for looks you would think that a sneeze would blow him away. With him you never have to worry. Just give him a job and you can forget about it. He dopes out all the angles and always works on his own."

Alan's voice shook.

"What does he use, Joe? A gun? A knife? Poison?"

"He uses whatever he thinks best for the job on hand. He likes accidents. Sometimes he likes illnesses. He knows more about drugs and poisons than most of the pill-pushers in the country. He knows everything about electricity. Some of the traps he's rigged up with ordinary house currents would honestly make you laugh."

Joe stood and walked over to a handsome jardiniere where, with well-bred aplomb, he spat.

"How is your wife's health, Al?" he said.

"Fine."

"Is her ticker okay?"

"She is strong as an ox."

"Well, the Dove will know best."

"I—I wouldn't have to know a thing about this, Joe?"

"You could put it right out of your head until it was time to be surprised and shocked. You wouldn't have to turn a finger beyond ordering the blanket of roses and a wreath. That is the nice part about the Dove—once you turn him loose on a job, you never see him again until it's over. The whole Missing Persons Bureau couldn't contact him if they wanted to. Even I couldn't. He works like a ghost."

Alan's superb tan was a mottled, sickly gray. It would be a break in a million to have the old crock safely shuffled off and a good-sized fortune in his hands. But was it worth it? The risk? Basically he was a coward, certainly a physical one. At Christine's sudden death he would instantly become Suspect Number One, unless the Dove were to do a superhuman job of camouflaging. "Would he do it here? Right in the house, Joe?"

"He might. Plenty of old women slip in their bathtubs or fall downstairs. At times they fall out of windows. Maybe there's a short circuit in some electrical gadget in their bathrooms. Accidents happen inside of houses. All with results."

"If it were poison—they're awfully clever with their autopsies, Joe."

"With the Dove there is no autopsies. And whatever it is, he will do it soon. I am worried about her maybe changing her will." He gave Alan a comprehensive look. "I want the job settled before Christine gets time to think you over."

Although teetering on the brink, it was no go. The ham in Alan dramatized too vividly the denouement. "No, Joe—I can see it too plainly—"

"You can see what?"

"The final scene—every grisly bromide of it—the last long mile, the little green door, the chaplain, the audience of reporters and special guests, the shaven head, the slit in the pants—No, Joe. I say no."

Joe said with amiable logic: "You have nothing to say about it. Which would you rather be? A widower or a corpse?"

The last vestige of color fled Alan's smooth cheek. "Would there be anything more than the twenty-five thousand, Joe?"

Joe brushed this jejune naïveté negligently aside. "There will be an added expense or two. We can talk that over afterward."

Joe walked over to a spinet desk. Several silver frames stood on it containing portraits, one of which was of Christine. Joe took this from the frame and replaced the empty frame on the desk among the others.

"This is a better picture of your wife than the one in the papers."

Alan, now that the die was cast, had started to re-bound. A hint of his dazzling, golden future began to thrill him.

"It's the rig she slew them with one year at the Beaux Arts Ball. She went as Hecate—replete with torch and hound. But only one head."

Joe folded the picture once and put it in a coat pocket. "I'll take it along with me," he said. "It will simplify matters for the Dove."

"I'm beginning to get the feel of this, Joe. For the past year I've been stifled. Just a bonded slave being stifled. It's like ozone. A great big breath of fresh ozone."

"There are one or two more things the Dove had better know. How about neighbors? Any patrols of any kind?"

"We could be in the middle of the Sahara."

"How much of the house is closed up?"

"All of it except for this wing, and most of this is too. We use this room generally as a gathering place."

"Where does your wife sleep?"

Alan indicated a door in the south wall.

"In there. There's a foyer that used to be a powder room, and a larger room beyond which she turned into a bedroom. A bathroom is connected with it."

"How many ways are there of getting into it?"

"Only by that door. The others were blocked up when she had the rooms done over."

Joe went to the foot of a small turret stairway in one corner.

"Is this the only stairway?"

"Joe, this rococo dump has at least twelve staircases."

"How about the top floor of this wing?"

"Just a residence for rats."

Joe indicated a small door set in a jog by the turret stairs.

"Coat cupboard?"

"It was. Christine had it made into a quick-freezer locker room. She uses it to store her furs."

"This is important, Al."

"What is?"

"Does your wife have any habits?"

"She is filled with them."

"I mean special ones—things that nobody else does in the house but herself."

"She plays that damned clavichord whenever she feels like it. Nobody else can play a note, if that's any good to you."

Joe thoughtfully looked at the clavichord, which had its keyboard facing and close to a wall. He looked at the chair-backed stool on which the player would sit. His eye briefly traveled up to the stuffed head of a tusked wild boar, set on a heavy oval plaque, which hung on the wall directly above this chair.

"You never can tell," he said. "One of the Dove's specialties is vibrations. How about liquor?"

"Well, she drinks, of course."

"Anything special? Just used by her?"

"Yes, Joe, there is. It's a cordial—Prunelle. There's a bottle of it in the cellaret. It's the only one left, and she'd cut the hand off anyone who touched it."

Joe went to the french door and opened it.

"So long, Al. Don't bother to see me around front." Alan seized one of Joe's hands and gripped it.

"Joe, I can't begin to tell you what this means to me."

"Glad to oblige, Al."

"Free! No more servitude to the whims of age! Joe, Edmond Dantes must have felt like this."

"What was his racket?"

"He was the Count of Monte Cristo. From chains to riches!" Alan dipped into the practical: "You will see the Dove right away, Joe?"

"He will be on his way here before dark. Don't worry, Al. Christine is as good as cooked."

Alan stepped out onto the terrace after Joe had gone. Now that there was no retreat, he simply dropped the asbestos curtain on the whole unsavory venture. His ability to do this in any situation, no matter how upsetting, never failed. Hugo had noticed this power in him and had been interested. Hugo had said something about glands.

A mountain breeze gently cleared Alan's head and brought him a sense of exhilaration and power. He idly decided that the breeze would die at nightfall and that a fog in all probability would set in. Most suitable indeed.

He left the flagged terrace and walked over a carpet of pine needles to the shore of the little lake. An intoxication of release filled him, for his mind accepted the job as being already as good as done. Fate, in the sleekly sinister person of Joe, had opened a dizzying vista of golden freedom.

He considered it fantastic that his station in life should have altered so in a minute, and through no volition of his own, but it was no more than just. What was that odd remark which Joe had made about the Dove?

He works like a ghost.

Alan savored the phrase with intense pleasure. It cast the horrendous plan into the regions of the unreal, made of murder an unseen wraith which in its own thoughtful time would separate from the shadows of some dust-sheeted portion of the house and silently, cleverly envelop Christine.

He was, by now, a combination of Tarzan, Superman, and John D. Rockefeller. He took a deep lungful of the cool, crisp mountain air. He pounded his magnificent chest. The ham in him reached its full flavor.

"The world," he cried triumphantly to the indifferent mountains, "is mine!"

CHAPTER III

Christine's hair, this year, was red.

She had tried several shades and had settled on titian. The effect was a frank and startling one. She wore this lambent hair in the latest mode, and in certain lights it tinged her face with the macabre, an effect which did little to relieve her features from the traces left by the years.

The features in themselves were well shaped and leaned toward what is generally considered as the aristocratic. Her figure was excellent, being slender and erect, and her clothes were designed by one of New York's best houses to give her great individuality and style. They invariably caused most women who came in contact with her to feel dowdy and to dislike her on sight.

As Christine's car moved along with the traffic of lower Broadway her intelligently wicked violet eyes were speculative on the back of Hugo's neck. It was a stocky neck, in keeping with his general compact build, and its skin would turn the shade of a ripe watermelon whenever Hugo was more than normally annoyed. It was that color now.

Hugo stopped the car at the entrance to a towering building in which Stuyvesant Swain, Christine's lawyer, had his-offices. Hugo helped Christine out. His lips were compressed into a thin, vitriolic line. He had been telling himself all the way in from Dour Notch the precise phrases in which he would ask Christine to go to hell and take her beneficences along with her.

Hugo's sole passion lay in experimentation with roentgeno-therapy. He was a callous, thoroughly cynical man who would cheerfully have used his own grandmother as a guinea pig if he had required her to further his work. Life and death meant literally nothing more to him than phenomena arranged through the offices of some natural force for the benefit of his scientific inspection.

Christine's decision to have him drive her into New York ("You won't mind doing this little thing for me, will you, Hugo?") just as he was involved in a compelling problem had forced Hugo into a fury.

Christine smiled at him appealingly and looked her most helpless.

"Before you pick the car up and hurl it at me, Hugo, why not run uptown and order that machine, or whatever it is, you spoke about the other day? I shall be hours with Stuyvesant. You could meet me at the Ambassador at five."

The watermelon color drained from Hugo's skin, leaving it pale. He thought: What a devil she is! Truly one.

The "machine, or whatever it is" which she now tossed him like an appeasing bone was an instrument far beyond his own negligible means to possess. It would help his work signally.

He knew it to be the sort of gesture which Christine always held in reserve for use when her subjects grew balky. Such as the gesture of her marriage yesterday to Alan. Hugo was satisfied that sex hadn't entered into it. She was finished with anything like that. No, it was simply that she would go to any extent rather than release a possession before she herself grew tired of it.

That these possessions were human beings did not matter. Neither Alan, nor Godfrey, nor Cordelia, nor himself.

He said calmly, "Thank you, Christine. That is very good of you. At five, then?"

"If you're sure you don't mind, Hugo?"

"No, Christine, I do not mind."

Stuyvesant Swain's offices were on the forty-third floor. They consisted of a reception room, three rooms for his junior associates, and what amounted to a salon for himself. This chamber was large and chaste, and its windows gave a stunning view of the harbor and of Battery Park.

He stood up as Christine came in and walked over to greet her. Ever since Charley's death had left her in control of the Belder fortune he had given it up as stupid to become upset by Christine's antics. He wished he could understand her. She was so completely different from anyone else whom he had ever known that she fascinated him. She'd get it in the neck, of course, eventually. This latest stunt of marrying that fortune hunter who was young enough to be her grandson might well turn out to be the final outrage.

"So you really did it," he said, taking one of her gloved hands and leading her to a chair.

She settled herself comfortably, arranged her furs as an effective frame for her face. She reminded Stuyvesant of a portrait sketch he had seen of Sarah Bernhardt done by Whistler. Or had it been an Aubrey Beardsley? Something just as exciting, but decadently so?

"Alan was growing restive," Christine said. "What else could I do?"

"I don't mind telling you I kept hoping some last minute bolt from the blue would bring you to your senses."

"Bolts from the blue no longer impress me, Stuyvesant. I bat them right back."

Stuyvesant stood looking down at her.

"I'll never understand you, Christine. God knows why Charley ever married you."

"He loved me."

"Yes, I know he did, poor devil. I can almost see him spinning in his grave over this latest outrage."

"Marrying Alan wasn't an outrage. It was the most convenient anchor at hand."

"Are you sure it was worth it? You know what it means, of course."

"Ostracized by my friends?" Christine smiled briefly. "What friends? They were Charley's really. Ones veneered on him by his family. Has it never occurred to you that such friends are a form of bondage?"

In a way he could see that for Christine such a viewpoint would be true. Mentally he slid over the roster of families who had been Charley's friends and who, after his death, had perforce continued to be friends with Christine. To the extent which she would permit. They were sterling. They were sound. And they were a dull lot from the very monotonies of their routine of living. He went behind the desk and sat down.

"I suppose you are here to change your will? Now that you've got him?"

Christine succeeded in looking shocked and faintly offended.

"I should think you would know me better than that, Stuyvesant."

He studied her speculatively, wondering whether after all she *had* gone slightly soft in the head and had truly fallen for that twirp. Women of Christine's years were famous for it. They got to the point where they would believe anything, no matter how thickly it was slathered on.

But if not the will, what then? What was she here for? An unpleasant thought came that she might intend to set the fellow up with a personal fortune. Poor Charley! Stuyvesant had been fond of Charley.

He wondered whether it would do any good to pump a scare into Christine. Whether it would be possible to pump one. If it were strong enough, he might even get her to divorce the scoundrel before any harm was done. He had a supreme distaste for melodramatics (his practice lay exclusively in the placid management of large and equally placid estates), but in Christine's instance wasn't he justified? Was there not a *genuine* danger against which she should be warned and sheltered? Surely he owed it to Charley's memory.

"Look here, Christine," he said, "has it never struck you that for some time you've been heading for trouble?"

"I fail to see how, Stuyvesant."

He tried not to become impatient.

"I am talking about these various groups of alleged friends you have picked up and discarded since you settled down at Belder Tor. Settled!"

"My motives have always been of the kindest, Stuyvesant. I've helped them to the extent of my modest ability, and they have amused me."

"I'm not questioning your motives. I simply shudder. But I am questioning your common sense. Take that mess with the Laura Destin woman. All you did in that instance was to receive into your home a potential homicidal maniac."

"That is ended."

"A situation of that sort is never ended. Diseased minds such as Laura Destin's brood. They never let up. And now this!"

"You mean Alan?"

"I do. You don't imagine that he married you for your violet eyes, do you?"

"Evidently you don't know me as well as I thought you did."

"That's better." Stuyvesant gestured irritably. "I have always detested melodramatics. You know that."

"And I, darling, adore them."

"I know you do." He said in exasperation: "Christine, surely it must have occurred to you that women with far less money than yourself have been murdered for it by the fortune hunters who have married them?"

"Certainly it has. I've always been fascinated by the more celebrated cases in the past. Landru, I should say, is my favorite."

Stuyvesant regarded her helplessly. She must be invincibly sure of herself and of her hold over that popinjay, or else he (the popinjay) must be a sorrier and more spineless lot than Stuyvesant had judged from his press picture. Stuyvesant had little liking for Christine, certainly no fondness, but he still felt that deep obligation to protect her because of Charley. Charley (God knew why) had been crazy about her.

She was up to some mischief right now. She had that demure look of a trusting, guileless child. Guileless!

He said, "Well?"

"I came about an annuity."

A look of unwilling respect spread across Stuyvesant's face.

"Christine, this is the most fiendish scheme you have ever cooked up during your lifetime of fiendish schemes."

She said meekly, "Thank you, Stuyvesant."

"Naturally you had no intention of changing your will! There would be no need for it. By sinking all your holdings into an annuity there will be nothing but negligible assets left to bestow, while you yourself will draw a large and tax-exempt income for the rest of your life. Do you know that I am almost tempted to feel sorry for that young poison adder?"

"And I shall live to be a hundred."

"I bet you will. If for no other purpose than to confound the insurance companies who handle the deal."

"And so safely, Stuyvesant."

"I know, and for Charley's sake thank God. It is only *by* living that you will be worth a cent to anybody. Not only to that virulent mountebank but to all the rest of the satellites you bedizen yourself with. Kill you, and the golden eggs die too. Christine, in this menacing situation an annuity offers a solution of positively asp-like genius. You will let him know of it, of course?"

Christine looked smugly virtuous: an elderly, well-preserved saint done in tinted plaster.

"I tell Alan everything. I will let him know this evening when I get home. Dear Alan! We will have so much more money to spend. My income will be larger under an annuity, won't it, Stuyvesant?"

"Considerably."

He was swept along with his own forebodings. Possibly the darkling day, with its brooding hints of fog, had a good deal to do with lifting the moment from its bedding of outrageous melodrama and into the fields of reality.

He foresaw exigencies: an accident arranged for the car, a welcoming drink on her arrival back at Belder Tor: a chalice tendered by a solicitous Alan in which would lurk the incipience of some subtle manner of death.

"Christine, we will do this as rapidly as possible. I *think* I can arrange to settle it by this afternoon, at least to the extent of giving you immediate coverage. The amount of the policies will be large enough to tempt them into a reasonable haste. Other details can be left until later, but at least you will be safe."

"Surely we mustn't take this *too* seriously, Stuyvesant."

"We must! I want you to call that young scorpion up on the telephone and tell him about it right now."

"But I *can't* call up a new husband and just casually announce that I've turned my money into an annuity."

Stuyvesant pressed a handkerchief to his brow. "No, I suppose that would be too much even for you. But tell him the instant you get home, and take every reasonable precaution on the drive back to Belder Tor." He flipped the switch of an annunciator on his desk, and a girl's voice said: "Yes, Mr. Swain?"

"Get me Rollins of the Mercantile Trust."

"Yes, Mr. Swain."

"If he's in conference, have them get him out. It's important. Vitally so."

"Stuyvesant," Christine said, "control your nerves. You're beginning to scare yourself stiff."

CHAPTER IV

Lida Belder was a pleasant-faced, wholesome young thing of eighteen, and one good look at her would assure you that her interests would promptly identify themselves with any of the more laborious charitable projects of the Junior League. They would fall, in fact, just short of an absorption in puppets.

Wind whipped the sensible handkerchief that guarded her hair as Barry Vanbuskirk drove his roadster beneath the saturnine sky of late afternoon through the infernoesque chasm of Dour Notch.

"Dank," she said, "isn't it?"

Barry looked at Lida fondly. He was a spindly but wiry young man of about twenty, and the prototype of any minor official in a good banking house manned by graduates of Groton and Harvard. His features were pleasant enough, even though they successfully concealed the fact that he was anything but dumb.

"At any minute now," he said to Lida, "I expect to be pelted with gnomes."

She rested her hand for an affectionate moment on his. She wondered whether her grandaunt Christine would be difficult. Curiously, she felt that any difficulty would arise not so much from a consent to her engagement and hoped-for swift marriage to Barry as it would from the mere act of her coming, without either encouragement or invitation, to Belder Tor at all.

She never had been, because Christine had always managed that their meetings and brief visits take place at Christine's apartment in New York. Christine had always puzzled her, and dazzled her too, and Lida thought of her as a hummingbird which never aged any more than had Rider Haggard's *She*.

Her own and Barry's impression of Belder Tor (when it frightened them starkly face to face) was a good deal akin to what Joe Inbrun's had been. Barry parked the roadster and they got out. Barry got and carried Lida's bags.

He said, "This is something simply out of Disney." They walked up the shallow granite steps. Barry found and pushed a button. After a while he pushed it again. "Let's look for a back door," Lida said.

"If we can find one before dropping through an oubliette."

They skirted the granite mass and saw one of the french doors of the morning room standing open. They went into the empty, silent room.

"Your telegram," Barry said, "will probably be delivered here next week by the Headless Horseman." Lida had been looking around. She went to the spinet desk. A Western Union envelope was propped against an inkwell.

"Here it is, Barry. It isn't opened."

Barry, too, had been looking around.

"What do we do now?" he asked. "Yell?"

Lida saw a bellpull. She pulled it. She said, "I'll ring."

"Lida, if one panel slides we duck."

"I don't see any panels, darling. I suppose the servants' quarters are a mile away."

A handset telephone on the spinet desk started ringing. For the first ring or two, Barry and Lida simply looked at it. It kept on ringing.

Barry went over and picked it up.

"That's one thing," he said, "that does get on my nerves."

"It might be Aunt Christine."

Barry said into the phone: "Hello?" He turned to Lida. "It isn't. It's a man's voice. Pompous type. Sounds something like a bullfrog through an amplifier." He said into the phone: "I beg your pardon, sir, I didn't get that. I was talking to Miss Belder. That's right, Lida Belder." Barry covered the mouthpiece. "Lida, he knows you."

"Then it must be Stuyvesant Swain, Aunt Christine's lawyer. He's the only one of her friends I know."

"It is." He uncovered the mouthpiece. "I'm Barry Vanbuskirk, Mr. Swain."

Barry gagged faintly and said to Lida: "I think he's crazy. He just said: 'One of the menagerie, I presume?'"

"He isn't crazy a bit. He's very nice. He takes me to a matinee of *The Barber of Seville* once a year."

"I bet he gives you tea afterwards. And cinnamon toast."

"Yes, he does."

"Sorry, Mr. Swain," Barry said into the phone. "Lida keeps interrupting me. Well, Lida didn't expect to be here herself. She came here because of me. We're engaged. Yes, Barry Vanbuskirk, that's right. Yes, that's right too. Back Bay."

Barry covered the mouthpiece and said: "He wants to know if we're the Boston Vanbuskirks. Old snob. If this thing were television I'd open a vein."

"He *isn't*, darling. He's just stuffy and nice."

Barry returned to the telephone: "It's for inspection, sir. Lida needs her grandaunt's consent before we can get married. Very kind of you, sir. Yes, it is fairly sudden, but I've only a week before induction. I know four sentences in German, so they've decided to make me a tenth assistant to a minor aide for the occupation. No, Mother and Dad aren't with us, but they're coming by train to New York, probably tomorrow. I'm meeting them and driving them out. I'm the only one in the family who's got any gas. I think the purpose of their coming is that the inspection be mutual—I'm sure you know parents, sir. I don't believe Mrs. Admont is here. Nobody seems to be here. Lida's wire to her is still unopened on the desk. Really?"

Barry said to Lida: "He says *that* doesn't mean a thing. He seems upset. He asked if she'd reached here safely." Barry listened, then said: "Around seven o'clock, sir? Yes, I will. No, I'm not sure I'll be here, sir. Lida will stay at Belder Tor, of course, but I'm putting up at the inn at Dour Notch. Just as a footnote, they use cerements for sheets. Yes, either I or Lida will give Mrs. Admont your message as soon as we find her. Good-by, Mr. Swain." Barry hung up. He said to Lida: "He's driving out here around seven. He sounded as though he were in a sweat about something."

"I wonder if anybody *is* in the house."

"We might try the cellar. We could start with digging up the cement. That's where they usually bury them."

"Oh, Barry! It is pretty grim, though, isn't it?"

"I have been in gayer spots, dear. The Boston morgue, to name one. Lida, a good harrowing scream and seven clanking chains would get no attention around here whatsoever."

A door in the north wall opened suddenly and Godfrey Lance came in. Godfrey was a man in his forties, completely fattened by a lifetime of gourmandizing, utterly self-centered, and with a voice which he felt commandingly established his own sense of importance. He had been baking petits fours, and chalk-white flour streaked his face where he had wiped it.

Godfrey glanced negligently at Lida and Barry and started up the turret stairs. Before he was quite out of their sight he stopped and ran down to them again. He walked over to Lida and looked at her through slitted eyes.

Barry said to her: "Draw a circle around yourself quick and say abracadabra three times."

Godfrey ignored this. He ignored Barry. He said to Lida: "I shall paint you. Have you any money? But of course you have. You have the patina of riches. I shall do your flesh in green. Not the stupid fragility of springtime, but with a sturdier, lettuce touch. You have the qualities of Mother Earth. A burgeoning. Your psychoses will hover around in a background. Tomorrow I shall find out what they are."

Godfrey was finished with Lida. He boomed fiercely at Barry: "I paint!"

"I hoped it was only that."

Godfrey wasted no more time on them. He ran up the turret stairs.

"This *must* be Aunt Christine's house," Lida said. "I mean, the telegram is here."

"If that's a sample of her guests, I wouldn't call it a house. It's a home for old ectoplasms."

"Aunt Christine is simply over-individualistic. I like her, Barry, and you'll like her too."

"What earthly difference does it make? I mean to us?"

"Well, it would make a difference if she said no. Three full years, Barry."

"Don't worry. I'll like her and she'll like me, even if I have to play Josephine to every Napoleon who pops."

"But her friends *aren't* crazy, darling. It's just that Aunt Christine is amused with unusual people and likes to have them around her. There's never any harm in them. She explained it all to me two summers ago when she drove me up to stay with Peggy Towner at Martha's Vineyard."

Godfrey was suddenly with them again, running down the tur-ret stairs, a dirty piece of paper in his hand, which he waved at them.

"A boiled icing," he boomed, "the secret of which was divulged to me by a decrepit and utterly penniless countess from Vienna."

Barry did his best to block him.

"I wonder whether you would let Mrs. Admont know that we are here?"

Blocked, Godfrey came to a standstill and looked down on this pest. He had been bothered by innumerable telephone calls during the day from reporters wanting interviews with the bridal couple, and had further ruined Alan's reputation to a local correspondent of the Kingston *Star* who had called in person earlier in the after-noon. These two ganglings were, he now decided, another pair. He was sick of the lot of them.

"Christine," he said, "has not yet come back from town, and Alan is upstairs asleep. I think he is in a stupor. I think he is drunk. You are another reporter? Well, right now I have not the time to repeat my impressions of that half-baked Hamlet. I am arranging petits fours. Come back again."

Godfrey managed a by-pass toward the door and had almost reached it when the sound of an automobile horn was heard. It was a French horn, and the effect was one of an elegant chord in G.

"Wait!" Godfrey said. "There is Christine now. It is constitu-tionally impossible for her to arrive at this bat's hangout without a fanfare and having the red carpet rolled out."

He hurried from the room to welcome Christine, and Barry said: "Lida, I'm beginning to wonder."

"About what, darling?"

"Whether it's safe for you to stay here."

"Barry, don't be absurd."

"It isn't absurd. After all, the current incumbents are probably immune to walking illustrations out of Freud, but you're not."

"Darling, I'll call you at the inn at the very first brandish of a carving knife."

"Or the wave of a garrote?"

"Even the flick of one."

"Dear, don't look now, but here's another. Probably Queen Victoria."

Cordelia Banning was coming down the turret stairs. Cordelia was elderly, quite plump, and insatiably calm: the aunt type, with soft gray hair, smooth rosy cheeks, and almost moistly kind eyes. She became aware of Barry and Lida and said: "Good afternoon. I'm afraid we didn't hear the door chimes. We never do. I'm Cordelia Banning. I did hear Christine's car and came down to welcome her. Dear Christine, she loves to be welcomed."

"I'm her grandniece, Miss Banning, Lida Belder."

"Oh, my dear, welcome—Christine will be so happy."

"This is Barry Vanbuskirk."

They shook hands, and Christine swept into the room, flanked on either side by Godfrey and Hugo.

Christine was saying to Godfrey: "Honestly, why I live on this deserted roost for eagles heaven alone knows." She spotted Lida and was, for a brief instant, jounced.

"Lida! Why, my dear—whatever on earth—" She clutched at her social wits and said: "I'm so glad to see you."

"They are," Godfrey announced with complete conviction, "two reporters from the capitalistic press." Lida went to Christine and kissed her.

She said, "Tell him I'm nothing of the sort, Aunt Christine."

"Dear, the only way to get along with Godfrey is to ignore him. But why aren't you with Alice Vanbuskirk at Bar Harbor?"

"I was until they wired Barry yesterday that he would be inducted next week."

Christine became conscious of the spindly and wiry-looking young man.

"Barry?"

"Alice Vanbuskirk's brother, Aunt Christine."

"But how nice!"

"How do you do, Mrs. Admont?" Barry said.

Christine offered her hand. "Mr. Vanbuskirk, not a thing makes sense, but I'm delighted you are here."

"Thank you, Mrs. Admont."

"The Catskills will depress you after Bar Harbor, but don't let it throw you. When Charles bought this shattering little mountain peak several decades ago, he was obsessed by Joseph Jefferson's portrayal of Rip Van Winkle. It took Belder Tor to get it off his chest."

"But I think it's terribly—impressive, Mrs. Admont."

Hugo said thinly: "All major disasters are impressive." Christine patted his arm.

"Hugo, how right you are."

She introduced. She blazoned Hugo briefly as a genius at roentgenotherapy and Godfrey at painting, while Cordelia was cacheted as a dear, sweet friend. She was still trying to uncover some faint light as to this sudden encampment of Lida's.

She said to Barry: "I suppose you had the usual difficulties over locating us in this wilderness?"

"Well, we did ask a dwarf for directions about ten miles back. All he could gibber was Dour Notch while his palsied finger practically boxed the compass."

"Darling," Lida said, "it wasn't nearly as bad as that." The light burst, and Christine speedily reviewed her knowledge of the Vanbuskirks: wealthy, on speaking terms with the Cabots, a governor, one embassy—not St. James, of course, but still an embassy. "'Darling'?" she said. "After all, Lida, when *you* say 'darling'—"

"I hate to spring this so suddenly, Aunt Christine, but Barry and I are engaged."

"Enchanting!"

Lida hugged her.

"Then you don't mind?"

"Mind! My dear child, you don't know the relief"—Christine pulled herself together—"the relief it is to realize that this happiness has come to you."

"It's more than just an engagement, Mrs. Admont," Barry said. "Lida and I want to get married before next Friday."

"Friday?"

"That's when I'm to be inducted. Lida brought me down here to put me on exhibition and ask your consent."

"You *will* give it," Lida said. "Won't you, Aunt Christine?"

"Fervently. I married Charles at precisely your age, and he was perfectly able to endure it up to four years ago. Influenza. Friday—I must call up St. Thomas's—"

"Lida and I thought we'd just settle for a justice of the peace, Mrs. Admont," Barry said.

"Undoubtedly more sensible. There would hardly be time for anything else. I remember that Charles and I were married in

Mullinville, Kansas, by a man who lisped. Are those your bags, Lida?"

"Yes, Aunt Christine."

"Haven't you any, Mr. Vanbuskirk?"

"I'm staying at the inn, Mrs. Admont. I left them on the way out."

"So sorry. Hugo dear, do you mind taking Lida's bags upstairs? Put them in the room next to Cordelia's. I hope you don't object to field mice, Lida. We reek with them."

Hugo picked up the bags. He said: "This house is nothing short of a paradise for Frank Buck." He went up the turret stairs.

Christine's efficient eye settled on Cordelia. She suggested that Cordelia go up with Hugo and see that the room was put in shape. ("You don't mind, do you, dear?") She slid over Godfrey with the thought that it was time for him to be in the kitchen about dinner. She was herself beginning to feel somewhat exhausted from her active day. She eyed Youth biliously after Cordelia had gone and said: "Do sit down, children, or pour yourselves a drink or something."

"I'm really due back at the inn, Mrs. Admont," Barry said. "I arranged a little tea for Lida as our lunch was caught on the fly like a brass ring. I hoped you wouldn't mind?"

"We've so much to plan Aunt Christine," Lida said.

Christine pressed fingertips to her tired eyes.

"I can think of nothing more agreeable."

"The food at that inn," Godfrey boomed. "Inn? In that decalcomania for a Swiss chalet—would disgust a mink."

"Godfrey," Christine asked, "where is Alan?"

"He sleeps."

"When do we dine?"

"At eight. We are having pheasant *a la chasseur*. Right now I ice the petits fours. You have had welcome enough."

Godfrey left the room, and Christine said: "Bring Lida back in time for dinner, Barry, and you must join us too."

"Thank you. Mr. Swain telephoned, Mrs. Admont. He is driving here to see you at seven."

"Dear Stuyvesant!"

Well, Christine wondered, why don't they go? She wanted to take off her things, to soak in a good warm tub, to relax. How awkward Youth was with partings. She heard Barry saying: "I hope you won't think this odd, Mrs. Admont, but Friday *is* such a short time away—"

"I think nothing is odd, dear boy, except those things which fall within the bounds of reason."

"It's about Mother and Dad. They're most anxious to meet you."

"They're coming down from Bar Harbor," Lida said, "and Barry's driving in to pick them up tomorrow, Aunt Christine."

"You must bring them at once to Belder Tor. Luncheon—dinner—whenever they happen to arrive. I shall be delighted."

"That's awfully kind of you," Barry said.

"Now run along, both of you. And I do hope you live through that tea at the inn."

"Until dinner then, Aunt Christine," Lida said.

"Be here for cocktails at half-past seven. Alan is working through a bar book I picked up several years ago at Cannes, and I think that tonight we're due for Number Twenty-nine."

CHAPTER V

Twilight fell on the sullen, overcast afternoon, and the light outside the french windows of the morning room became a vague chiaroscuro of morbid mauves, while the illumination of somber lamps did little to mitigate Belder Tor's sepulchral atmosphere.

Cordelia came in carrying a small tray of canapés. She was a touch mellow, very happy, and she hummed a bar or two of Schumann's "The Happy Farmer" as she put the tray on the cellaret. Years ago (she refused to remember how many) it was thought that she had a voice, and Fraulein Bieblemann had taught the tune to her in that big, dear old house of Papa's on Madison Avenue which was now the establishment of a haggard dealer in antiques.

She selected one of the canapés and ate it, then she poured a good shot of Christine's delightful eight-year-old, hundred-proof scotch and downed it. She thought dreamily of Lida. Such a nice girl. Attractive and well-bred. Cordelia thought she would give her a present.

The telephone rang. Cordelia put down her empty glass and started leisurely toward the spinet desk. She had just picked up the set when Alan almost fell down the turret stairs in his haste to take the call. He thought it might be from Joe.

Alan felt fine. He had slept most of the afternoon and had wakened still very solidly enthroned in the Dumas tradition. Like the faintest mote on the background of his mind was the awareness that Christine was in the house and that the Dove, in his own ghostly time, would attend to her, and good. Alan had spoken with her briefly before starting to dress. He was in his shirt sleeves when the telephone had rung, and his tuxedo tie was still untied.

He all but snatched the receiver from Cordelia.

"I'll take it, Cordelia."

"Oh dear, I do hope Miss Belder and Mr. Vanbuskirk haven't decided to linger at the inn."

Alan said eagerly into the telephone: "Joe?" Evidently it wasn't. His face fell. "Oh."

"Godfrey has the pheasants in the oven," Cordelia went on placidly, "and he'll be furious if they're overdone."

"Please, Cordelia!" Alan returned to the phone. "Sorry, what was that? Mrs. Glendenning Vanbuskirk? Oh yes, Mrs. Vanbuskirk, this is the home of Mrs. Alan Admont, Belder Tor. Your son and Miss Belder ought to be here any minute. They had tea at the inn. Certainly. I'll ask him to phone you at the Plaza as soon as he comes. Good-by."

Alan hung up. He said: "It's that Boston prig's mother. She and his undoubtedly also-priggish old man are in New York at the Plaza. They want him to call them up."

"*No*, Alan, Barry's nice, and I think Lida is sweet. She reminds me of Cousin Janette before she married that impossible man from Troy. I am going to give her a present."

Alan went over to the cellaret.

"How about a quick one, Cordelia?"

"You know I never touch a thing before cocktails, Alan."

"And how! Straight?"

"Straight."

Alan poured two shots and gave her one.

"Did you get Miss Belder's room in shape?"

"Yes." Cordelia downed the drink. "Mice."

"Any rats?"

"No, just six mice. That poisoned wheat is marvelous."

"Poison!" Alan was shocked momentarily bug-eyed into recalling the Dove. He found himself dramatizing Christine's imminent death, in terms of the soundly cyanided mice. "I wonder if they suffer?"

"I doubt it, Alan. The wheat grains are such a lovely amethyst blue."

"Even so."

Alan inspected the ingredients which Cordelia had set out for the cocktails. Hugo came in on his way up to dress. He had been having a happy hour or two in the laboratory. Alan, who hadn't seen him since he had driven Christine home, noted the trace of a smile on Hugo's misanthropic face and was mildly astonished. It was so seldom that Hugo looked pleased.

"You must have had a pleasant day in town, old man," Alan said.

"I did." Hugo's smile slid into the smug. "That is, it was pleasant after I dropped Christine at her lawyer's." Alan's hand, holding the glass of scotch, gave a spasmodic jerk.

"What did she want with him, Hugo?"

"She didn't say."

A trickle of cold sifted across Alan's satiny skin.

"Was she there long?"

"Oh, several hours."

Obliquely, Hugo watched Alan stew. Serve the conceited young fool right (he thought) if she has changed her will. He went on up the turret stairs.

Alan absently finished his drink. He felt suddenly nervous. Had Joe been right in his contention for the need of haste? Had Christine changed her will with this unmannerly swiftness (treachery, when you came right down to it) and cut him off without a cent before the Dove could get in his ashen work? Had all of this promise of splendor come too late?

He felt like rushing in and choking the truth out of Christine. No, that would never do. He must dissemble. He must furiously exert his charms (his self-assurance that he would have no difficulty in doing so greatly calmed him) and win her into changing it back. And on the other hand, this could well be but a teapot tempest he was stirring up. She often dropped in to sting the old buzzard about her investments. He felt serene again.

Faintly, from the distant entrance hall, came the sound of a door chime.

"Must be the niece and the prig," he said.

Alan ran up the turret stairs, fixing his tie as he went. Cordelia walked through a gloomy corridor to the entrance hall and opened the front door. Stuyvesant stood on the threshold.

"Good evening?" Cordelia said placidly.

"Good evening. I telephoned Mrs. Belder—Mrs. Admont—I find it impossible even to say that name! Anyhow, has she returned here as yet from the city? I am Stuyvesant Swain."

Cordelia closed the front door.

"Oh yes, Christine speaks about you so often, Mr. Swain."

"I can well imagine in what terms."

"I'm Cordelia Banning."

Stuyvesant accepted a soft, dimpled hand.

"Miss Banning. Would you be good enough to let Christine know that I am here?"

"Of course. Do come into the morning room. It's the only room in the house we ever use."

Stuyvesant put his hat and gloves on a console near the door. He shuddered, as he had always shuddered, at the suits of armor. Charley certainly had had the damnedest taste. He followed Cordelia into the morning room, where she left him and went into Christine's suite.

Nothing much, Stuyvesant decided, had changed. It had been years since he had been here. Since before Charley's death. But oh, good God, yes. He stood hypnotized before Christine's portrait.

Godfrey came in, carrying a steaming saucepan. Godfrey was pleased to see this well-dressed and expensive-looking stranger admiring his portrait.

"Do you like it?" Godfrey boomed. "It is my best."

"It's a—woman, isn't it?"

"It is Christine."

"You could be right at that."

"Where is Cordelia?"

"She went in there."

"Tell her when she comes out there will be time for one cocktail apiece. No more." Godfrey gave Stuyvesant a thoroughly menacing glower and said as he left the room, "Pheasants—*a la chasseur*!"

Stuyvesant, although scarcely surprised, did his best to orient himself in what he honestly considered to be a maniacal ménage. He raised his eyes to heaven and murmured, "Poor Charley!" as Christine came in with Cordelia.

Christine, very stunning in a simple and expensive dinner gown, gave him both her hands.

"Dear Stuyvesant! You are just in time for cocktails. Tonight we are due for Number Twenty-nine."

"Number Thirty, Christine," Cordelia said. "We had Twenty-nine last night. I remember the recipe—absinthe, brandy, and a dash of something which Hugo insisted was attar of Gila monster."

Stuyvesant said with considerable force: "Christine, a large maniac just burst through that door and told me to tell you we would only have time for one apiece. And thank God."

"That was Godfrey. Do find Alan, Cordelia, and say that any time now."

"He is just finishing dressing."

Cordelia went up the turret stairs.

Stuyvesant pressed a chastely monogrammed handkerchief to his brow. Godfrey's bravura had shaken him more than he had cared to admit.

He said, "Christine, I cannot begin to tell you the shock it was to me when I telephoned and found that you hadn't reached Belder Tor."

"But I must have, darling, almost immediately after." Stuyvesant went to the spinet desk and, taking a legal document from his pocket, spread it out. He took out his fountain pen and tested it.

"After you left," he said, "it was thought best to make a slight alteration in one of the clauses. It requires your initials. To a measure I was glad of it, as it gave me an excuse to drive up and see with my own eyes that you were safely home, and to assure myself that you had spiked that young reptile's fangs by telling him about the annuity. You have, of course?"

"No, Stuyvesant. Not yet. It *has* been such a day."

"Then thank God that I have come. I shall be in a fever of impatience until you do so—and if you don't I will. Initial this at once, Christine, right here."

He handed Christine the pen, and she sat down at the desk just as the sound of the door chime floated in. Christine stood up again.

"That must be Lida and Barry."

"*Sign your initials*, Christine!"

Christine started for the door.

"I will, darling."

Stuyvesant stewed until she came back. Lida and Barry were with her, and Lida was saying: "Such a lovely afternoon!"

"The meal was completely up to expectation, Mrs. Admont," Barry said. "Grilled flanks of Arabian chargers and flaccid potatoes baked in their shrouds."

Cordelia came down the turret stairs, followed by Alan and Hugo. Lida had gone over to Stuyvesant and was saying: "Good evening, Mr. Swain."

"Lida, my dear girl, I understand you are to be wished all happiness. Mr. Vanbuskirk? Congratulations."

"Thank you, Mr. Swain."

Alan, ever volatile, had found the crest of the wave ripped from under him when Cordelia had told him that Stuyvesant was in the house. Again he was certain that the old Beelzebub (female variety) *had* changed her will. His intention of furiously to dissemble was, in consequence, hitting on all cylinders. He smiled radiantly at Stuyvesant, whom he found practically facing him like a stolid, granite wall, and said: "Cordelia told me you were here."

"Mr. Admont, I presume?"

Alan seized and pumped Stuyvesant's hand.

"Christine and I both missed you at the wedding."

"Quite so."

Christine introduced him to Lida and Barry, and Alan continued in his role of the gracious host. Lida, now that she was face to face with him, was instantly struck (everybody always was) by Alan's good looks and build. Even though she had been prepared for his youth, for the chasm between the ages of himself and Christine, this visual proof of it affected her like a cataract of chill water. It was curious, she thought, how you could understand one of these spring-and-winter marriages when it was the man who had the frosting of ice. And how distasteful it was in reverse.

"Do pour cocktails, Alan," Christine said. "Godfrey's getting temperamental about the pheasants."

Alan went to the cellaret while Stuyvesant pointed significantly to the annuity on the desk and said: "Christine!"

"Right away, Stuyvesant. Have you met Dr. Wintersweet?"

Stuyvesant bowed to Hugo.

"How do you do, Doctor?"

"Hugo," Christine said, "is abysmally brilliant. He is experimenting with roentgen rays."

"During my odd moments, Mr. Swain."

"Very interesting, I'm sure."

Cordelia had joined Barry and Lida.

"Your mother telephoned, Mr. Vanbuskirk," she said. "She and your father are in New York at the Plaza and would like you to call them up."

"Thank you. I'll give them a ring from the inn after dinner."

"Call them up from here, Barry," Christine said. "The phone is on the desk."

"Thank you very much."

Christine took a cocktail from Alan, and Stuyvesant, with what definitely could be called anguish in his voice, said sharply: "Chris-*tine*!" He pointed again to the annuity.

"*Yes*, Stuyvesant."

Barry said into the telephone: "Will you connect me with Mrs. Glendenning Vanbuskirk, please, at the Plaza Hotel in New York?"

"Better hang on, Barry," Christine said. "I had Alan get Florida yesterday, and the call practically blew back in his face. Godfrey wanted stone crabs."

"I will, Mrs. Admont."

Stuyvesant, with considerable suspicion, accepted a cocktail from Alan.

"Number Thirty, I believe?" he said.

"That's right. Cognac, yellow chartreuse, and lime."

"The lime," Hugo said, taking one, "unquestionably is unslaked."

Cordelia offered canapés of an interesting brown-ball effect on toothpicks.

"Godfrey is outdoing himself," Hugo said, swallowing one.

"What are they?" Stuyvesant asked, swallowing one too.

"Snails."

It was too late.

"Do take one, Lida," Christine was saying. "They're the last snails out of Paris."

Barry's connection came through, and they heard him say: "Mother? Barry talking. Yes—yes, dear—certainly, if you wish it. I'll start after dinner."

Christine went over to the desk.

"Do let me talk to her, Barry."

"Mother—Mrs. Admont wants to speak to you."

Christine took the telephone.

"Mrs. Vanbuskirk? I'm Christine Admont. Barry tells me that you and Mr. Vanbuskirk will be with us tomorrow. I couldn't be more delighted. Do manage to reach here in time for luncheon or dinner, and plan to stay over. Oh? So sensible—and of course Lida will understand. Until tomorrow afternoon, then. Good-by."

Barry had joined Lida. He said to her: "Mother wants me to drive in tonight and stay with them at the Plaza."

"Oh, darling—if this wretched fog lifts there'll be a moon."

"They've been digging around Chelsea and have uprooted three aunts. I'm to take the role of the fatted calf."

"I hope each aunt gets indigestion."

"Christine," Stuyvesant said in a voice plainly meant to brook no further nonsense, "at once!"

He stood over her at the desk and pointed severely to the annuity. Christine put her initials on the indicated spot.

"There."

"At last!"

Stuyvesant picked the document up and waved it to dry the ink.

Ice swiftly clutched Alan's arrested heart. "What are you signing, darling?" he asked almost sharply.

"Not, at any rate, a new will," Hugo said. "No witnesses have been asked for."

Alan threw him a vicious look. He was thoroughly startled.

"Will? Christine—you haven't—you *wouldn't*—"

"How could you think such a thing of me, Alan? It is something else entirely. In fact, you will be enchanted. You might almost call it a present."

It was remarkable how Alan rebounded. The distressed front lifted, and he looked like a stroked and well-pleased cat.

"Really? But my birthday isn't until next month, darling."

"It isn't that sort of a present, darling."

Stuyvesant folded the annuity and put it in his pocket.

He announced to the room at large: "There is a word in the English language known as comeuppance."

"Christine," Hugo said, "a whiff of brimstone is sifting through the air."

"Dear Stuyvesant was so efficient, Alan. He had the whole thing put through in no time—physical examination—transfers—everything, so far as immediate coverage is concerned."

"Darling, what are you talking about?"

"An annuity, dear. For me."

The word dropped like a stone in the silent pool. Hugo gave a short laugh, while Alan turned an oyster gray. He looked as if he were about to faint.

"An annuity?" Cordelia said. "But what a good idea! It brings in so much more than any other type of investment, doesn't it?"

Stuyvesant said: "Yes." He glared pregnantly at Alan and added: "But only during the holder's lifetime."

"And," Hugo added further, "the insurance company hits the jackpot when Christine dies."

"Oh, but we mustn't think of *that,*" Cordelia said calmly.

Christine managed to make her eyes bewitchingly fond. She turned them on Alan. "We will have so much more to spend through the happy, happy years."

Alan felt as though he were strangling. He managed to blurt out: "Did you put everything into it? All? The whole thing, darling?"

"Everything but the jewels. I knew you would be pleased, dear."

"Come and get it, folks," Godfrey's bass voice bellowed from the doorway. "Pheasant—*a la chasseur*!"

Christine linked her arms with Barry's and Lida's. "I'm starving after the drive out."

"I'm starving," Barry said, "after that meal."

They followed Godfrey from the room. Cordelia walked after them with Stuyvesant.

"I remember now," she said, "that Victoria Swansbeck bought an annuity when she was fifty-four years old. She wanted to feel safe. I forget which depression it was during, but a day didn't pass without some stockbroker jumping out of a window."

Alan was still rooted to the spot. Hugo asked him, with wicked solicitude, "Won't you join us, Alan?"

"In a minute. I'll be right in."

"Take your time. If shock doesn't kill during the first few minutes, the chances are about fifty-fifty that the victim will recover."

"Oh, for God's sake, leave me alone!"

"I'll let them know you'll be right in."

Hugo presented Alan with his best Mephistophelean grin and left the room. Alan waited for a moment and then, swiftly as a cat, ran to the doorway and stood listening to the dying murmur of voices. He took the telephone from the desk and stood with its cord full-stretched so that, while phoning, he could keep an eye along the hall.

He gave the operator the number of Joe's penthouse in New York. His blood was alternately fever and ice. His hand shook as he held the receiver to his ear. He gave an almost convulsive sigh of relief when Joe's voice answered.

"This is Alan, Joe."

"Yes?"

"Something ghastly has happened. Something that affects you-know-what."

"Spill it."

"Christine saw her lawyer when she went into town. He's out here now. She has turned her entire fortune into an annuity, and the papers are signed."

There was, at Joe's end of the line, dead silence.

"Don't you see what that means?" Alan said frantically. "If she—if anything happens to her, I don't get a cent. The insurance company takes the works. You've got to cancel that deal. You've got to get hold of the Dove right away."

"You can't. I told you that this morning."

"I know you did, but you've *got* to get in touch with him. You've *got* to call him off!"

"For the last time, get this straight, Al. Not a soul on earth could put a finger on the Dove until this job is finished and he decides to show up and collect."

"But there won't *be* anything to collect. I can't let Christine be mur—Don't you see I've got to keep her healthy?"

"I cannot be more final, Al. He is on the job, and I told him it had to be done quick. You can start picking the hymns out right now. Tell me this. Did she turn in her jewels?"

"No. But what of it? Nowadays they probably wouldn't fetch more than fifty thousand."

"It will just about take care of the Dove and me." Alan started to scream the words and then remembered. He forced his voice back to a whisper.

"I should hope it would! It means that if I don't keep her alive I'll be penniless. Joe—Joe, for God's sake, don't you realize that Christine has just gone in to eat? The Dove might be poisoning her right now!"

"And that," Joe said coldly, "is your tough luck."

Joe hung up.

CHAPTER VI

The receiver of the telephone remained in Alan's palsied hand, still pressed against his ear, until the impersonal voice of the operator asked: "Are you still connected with your party, please?"

"No. No, thank you very much."

Alan set the phone back on its cradle. What could he do? What were the things which must be done? A parade of decisions was instant in his feverish mind: preventatives against this implacable, untouchable, undeniable force (the Dove) which had been loosed so properly for his benefit and which now was calmly busied in phantasmal occupations for his swift ruin. Definitely with all the ingratitude of a Frankenstein's monster.

Notes, Alan thought, could be left commanding the Dove to call the deal off. A note here, another one there, throughout the dust-sheet-shrouded empty spaces of the vast house. But was he in the house? And anyhow, notes were both silly and dangerous.

He wondered almost hysterically how he could address them (Dear Dove—Dear Mr. Dove?) and what he could ever say which would deter the Dove from accomplishing Christine's exit and which would still not incriminate Alan himself. He had a tremendous respect for the advisability of never putting a thing down in writing.

Whisk Christine away? Perhaps. But would she whisk? Alan thought not. And even so, where on this currently troubled earth could he take her to? Or what reason could he sensibly offer for a sudden evacuation of Belder Tor and headlong flight to parts unknown?

He dallied with the temptation of cutting it all out and himself decamping from the cruel and unfair mess. But what then? A distressing vista of such a future chilled Alan into revolt at the noisome thought. Rich old fools were few and far between these days.

It could be months, years even, of a horrid hall-bedroom existence before he could net another fish as financially gaudy as Christine.

And in any case would Joe be pleased if he were to skip?

Alan shuddered. It was a blank wall. All was despair except for the rigid necessity of keeping the old witch alive.

Self-pity overwhelmed him as he watched himself growing older year by year, saw the very best and ripest years of his life being frittered away in the irritating dullness of dancing attendance on a constantly disintegrating Christine.

Forty years at least. Alan (as well as Stuyvesant) was convinced that she would hit the century mark. Then (grim thought) he would be sixty-five, his good looks which were his stock in trade lost forever, and with nothing to show for it beyond such crumbs as he might have gathered from her opulent table and have salted away. He almost cried.

His head was desperately tired and his nerves were at the shattering point. Possibly the morning would bring some cogent plan which would fend off his ruin. A good night's sleep. *Dared* he sleep, and thus leave his now precious Christine wide open to heaven alone knew what shape or method of precarious attack?

On leaden feet Alan propelled his handsomely muscular body from the morning room and detoured through the entrance hall en route to join the others at Godfrey's succulent buffet.

The suits of armor which had usually amused him as being something out of simply nowhere now disturbed him. He knew the notion was full of the rankest corn and that the device had been thrown out into Shubert's alley, or its then equivalent, somewhere back in the days of Avery Hopwood, but just suppose the Dove *were* to be ensconced inside of one of them?

Absurd.

But is was not absurd to suppose that the Dove might be somewhere close at hand. ("I told him it had to be done quick," Joe had said.) How poorly the hall was lighted, with what spectral gloom! What bitter, dead-sea fruit the annuity made of the brilliant scheme right now.

Alan passed the foot of a dark stairway, then hesitated and turned back to it again. The upper hall, to his feverish eyes, was a stygian curtain threaded with vague shapes. No, there was nothing to see. No sound to hear.

But that (the blood in his remarkably healthy veins turned to ice) was, of course, the idea.

CHAPTER VII

A wind had sprung up and was sighing in its inscrutable passage through the pines. Hugo had started a log fire on the hearth, which added little more than a witch's note to the morning room's mortal, depressive tone. An hour had passed and the buffet was done.

Christine was seated on a lounge which, at the insistence of Charles, had been upholstered in royal purple. A large Sheffield tray with a silver service was on the coffee table before her. Alan was at her side. He watched her with the nervous anxiety of a mother hen, an anxiety which he was doing his best to conceal.

The others, almost as though under some ephemeral spell, were grouped: Lida, Barry and Godfrey near the hearth, Cordelia and Stuyvesant on a love seat (glumly petit-pointed) near the cellaret, while Hugo was sardonically observing them all as he stood leaning back against the clavichord, sipping his coffee.

Little could have been more depressing than the anecdote which Godfrey was just completing to Lida: "—which was, of course, back in nineteen thirty-seven. The miserable creature telephoned me at the Dome around midnight and said, 'Why go on?' I tell you that I wept!" Godfrey sighed gustily. "As a model she was superb—a new set of psychoses every time she posed."

"But what happened to her, Mr. Lance?"

Barry said, "There is always the Seine."

"Precisely," Godfrey boomed. "She died."

Alan all but choked on his coffee. "Died!… Are you sure your coffee tastes all right, Christine?"

"The flavor is perfect."

"The statistical rate of suicides in the Seine River," Stuyvesant said pompously, "used to be enormous."

"Something on your mind, Alan?" Hugo asked.

"No!"

Cordelia said with placid vagueness: "I wonder whether there's a storm in the air? There's a feeling of tension. I always remember how storms would affect dear Mabel Potash. At times they would give her fits."

"Some more coffee, Stuyvesant?" Christine asked.

"No more, thank you." He stood up. "Christine, I shall say good night."

Stuyvesant felt as satisfied as he could be. Christine still, it was true, was surrounded by her entourage out of Dementia, but at least the fangs of the most virulent one of them had been pulled. With a touch of irritation he shoved aside a coffee spoon that Godfrey poked under his nose.

"You are a foolish man," Godfrey was saying, "not to let me paint you. The portrait would remain famous long after you are dead."

"Must we," Alan asked with a sickly grin, "keep harping on such cheery notes as suicide and death, Godfrey, old man?"

"I do not harp. I state ah unequivocal fact."

"What color would you do Mr. Swain in, Godfrey?" Cordelia asked.

"Puce. Against pink moneybags floating on wings of steel."

"You're lucky, sir," Barry said to Stuyvesant. "Mr. Lance is contemplating immortalizing Lida as a head of lettuce."

"Christine," Stuyvesant said, "again good-by."

Barry stood up and joined him. "You have to pass the inn, sir. Will you give me a lift? We left the car there after that equine tea."

"With pleasure, Mr. Vanbuskirk."

"See you tomorrow," Barry said to Lida. He looked around the moribund room and shuddered. "I hope."

"I'm going to see you off."

"Thank you for coming out, Stuyvesant," Christine said as she and Alan walked with him toward the door.

"It was my duty." Stuyvesant gave Alan a good, sound glare. "It will always be my duty to guard your interests, Christine. For poor Charley's sake."

Cordelia stood up. She gazed fondly after Barry and Lida as they followed Christine and Alan and Stuyvesant out of the room. She said: "I love young love."

"Its effect on me," Hugo said, "is comparable to an incurable attack of *mal de mer*."

"Hugo," Godfrey boomed, "you should give up eating tomatoes. Your system is full of acid. I knew a man in Paris who switched to alligator pears and became a positive optimist."

Cordelia was busy with her skirt, which was cut rather full and of a lovely lilac-colored velvet. She reached a dimpled hand among its folds and, from one of its numerous inner pockets, took out a necklace of aquamarines. She looked at it and thought of Lida. Too gloomy. She returned the necklace and, selecting another pocket, took out a diamond clip.

"Would it occur to you," Hugo was saying to Godfrey, "that our young squirt has the wind up pretty badly?"

"He has been knocked flat by the news of Christine's annuity. I have no doubt but that he would eagerly have broken her neck, and now he must shelter her against the faintest pricking of a pin."

"And still I wonder."

"We must all be so careful of her now," Cordelia said. "We must be doubly kind." Her sweet eyes clouded. "Oh dear, I *do* hope the marriage won't make any difference. Alan does seem so restless. You don't suppose there will be a *change*? That our welcome—"

"Our welcome," Hugo stated flatly, "will remain good for the precise duration of the servant shortage."

Godfrey said, "To an extent you are right. We are safe as long as Christine remains here at Belder Tor. Her knowledge of cuisine does not remotely approach the purlieus of a boiled egg. Without me, she would starve."

Cordelia felt better. "And she never could make a bed. Or take care of the plumbing, Hugo, or drive a car. Dear Christine, she needs us so."

"A damn good thing for us that she does."

"I give you this," Godfrey boomed. "What if that conceited young ass—that parasitical, Westphalian crocodile—should persuade Christine to close Belder Tor and travel?"

"Nowadays?" Hugo asked. "Travel where?"

"What does it matter where? Anywhere away from this cenotaph to a bourgeois pork packer's misconception of a castle on the

Rhine." Godfrey turned to Cordelia. "Christine's first husband *was* a pork packer?"

"No Godfrey. Charles Belder was an engineer. Civil, I imagine."

"No matter. If I were not chained here as an economic slave, I would flee this monstrosity as the plague."

"Oh dear, I wouldn't. I do so hope you're wrong, Godfrey. Without Christine and Belder Tor, what would we do?"

"Die," said Hugo.

Christine came back with Alan and Lida. Christine was saying to Lida: "Barry is delightful. Later we must discuss a trousseau and a thousand things."

"I have everything I need, Aunt Christine."

"Undoubtedly. It's the things one doesn't need that are important."

"For you, dear," Cordelia said, going to Lida and handing her the diamond clip.

Lida was mildly stunned. "It's beautiful, Miss Banning. But why?"

"Because you remind me of my cousin Janette before she married that impossible man from Troy."

Alan said to Lida: "Cordelia is a unique phenomenon, in that she is a walking Christmas tree."

"A self-replenishing one, I might add," Hugo said.

"But this is much too expensive—too nice, Miss Banning," Lida said.

"My dear, it is the least I can do. Think of it as a little wedding gift."

"Lida," Christine said abruptly, "I have decided that any justice-of-the-peace business is absurd. There will be a very simple and informal ceremony here. Yes, the more I think it over—there's that minister at the Notch and the woman who sells eggs and sings—Godfrey can take care of the cake—the wedding march—" Christine looked speculatively at the clavichord. "I wonder whether the clavichord is in tune? I haven't played it for centuries." Definitely, Alan thought, my head is going to split. This puny chatter which rippled in wavelets of inconsequential tinsel across the mortal deep of his sable problem did its best, having entered one handsome ear, to go out the other, but most of it would stick, further stuffing his unusually crowded brain.

Clavichord? Wasn't that what the old crocodilian masterpiece had just said? It must have been, for she was moving toward the instrument with that walk of hers which was a combination of the determined aristocrat expertly coursing over knowledgeable seas and a vitality of spring outrageously lacking in a decent proportion to her years. And Joe—Joe had been interested—Joe had looked at the clavichord for an appreciable moment while storing it in his horrible mind as a possible murder instrument among the horrendous list compiled for the fog-like Dove.

How utterly absurd. But if so, Alan wondered, why am I sweating like a rain-drenched horse? He did his best to conceal the alarums which seemed to be screaming inside of him, and almost succeeded in smiling charmingly. Christine had reached the clavichord by now.

"Isn't it bad luck, darling?" Alan said.

"What, Alan?"

"To play the wedding march before the ceremony?"

"Not that I know of."

"Nor anybody else," Hugo said.

Christine went behind the instrument and sat down on the stool. Her back was very close to the wall.

"I simply want to find out whether it's in tune."

Lida went over and joined her.

"I've never heard a clavichord. Is it much different from a piano?"

"It is like striking the keys with mallets," Godfrey boomed. "And the tone is that of an intelligent dishpan."

Christine rippled a few chords in the treble register.

"You do have to hit the keys rather hard."

Alan's torture receded in a surge of relief. Just what diabolical confection he had been expecting he did not know. Something, fantastically, along the line of a violent explosion. But no. The Dove, according to Joe's advance press-agenting, was too subtle for anything as obvious as that. Poison? A poisoned pin point cleverly cemented on the ivory of a selected key? ("He knows more about drugs and poisons than most of the pill-pushers in the country," Joe had said.) The surge of relief fled, leaving in its sorry wake a tideless beach of insufferable poverty to mock Alan's haggard eyes.

"Darling, it is perfectly in tune." He furtively wiped his brow and added with fervor: "Perfectly!"

Christine tried a few more chords in the treble.

"The upper register is all right."

So far, Alan realized with a desperate snatch at the thought's tepid comfort, she hasn't *winced*. He watched her fingers in an agony of frustration as they moved to the center of the keyboard. Antidotes? But what was their use unless you knew the specific poison which had been introduced? Christine was tentative with a deeper chord, and still there was no wince.

But wait.

What *had* it been? On the fringe of Alan's vision something had moved. It had moved in response to the chord's fuller, more vibrant note. His eye shot upward along the wall to the heavy plaque (so conveniently hung directly above Christine's invaluable head) with its mounted wild boar's head and the dreadful, pointed tusks. More fearful even than a sword of Damocles, the potential murder weapon was in patient suspension. After one tremulous move?

His rich, red blood turned to water. What best to do? Snatch her swiftly, with the full strength of his magnificent arms, from the fatal stool? She would think him mad. All of them would—or, what was worse, some prescience might come to one of them which would betray, as a result of his inexplicable gesture, the unkind complicity of his secret guilt. As a convict about to be finitely juiced, Alan heard the reprieve of Lida's fresh young voice saying: "Do let me try it. May I?"

Christine stood up.

"It sounds something like one of those Russian things."

"Play their boat song, Lida," Cordelia suggested placidly. "One of Papa's dearest friends was a basso. So *triste*!"

Torture tightened its vicious clamp. Through an iced glaze of impotent inertia Alan saw the shift get under way. Could he—*could* he sacrifice this harmless young creature in the pristine bloom of love, of life itself, on the altar of his own so important and so urgent future? The question trembled and then died in its academic stage.

Then Christine paused.

The shift was still incomplete. The stool between them still empty. Christine struck a strong, harsh chord in the bass. The boar's head fell and shattered the fragile stool with a resounding crash.

And Alan screamed.

CHAPTER VIII

It was Hugo alone among them who noted Alan's scream and filed it away for further thought. The others had lost it in the general melee of their own shocked reactions.

The wretched scream had barely died on Alan's lips when he replaced it with a shout of: "Christine—are you all right? Did it touch you?" He ran to her.

"Yes—quite all right—Lida?"

Alan brushed any consequences to Lida aside and all but clung, in a restrained, hovering fashion, to Christine, whom he was convinced nothing but a miracle had preserved. He was obscurely conscious of Lida's: "No, it never touched me," and of Cordelia's placid comment that it must have weighed a ton.

"Odd," Hugo was saying, "that after all these years it should have chosen this evening—"

Hugo left the acid implication floating lightly in air, and Godfrey said: "Choose? How could a stuffed symbol of the overprivileged classes such as that thing *choose*?"

"You are *sure* you are all right, darling?" Alan implored.

"Perfectly, Alan—a little shaken—"

Lida was somewhat aghast. "Aunt Christine—if I hadn't asked you to let me play—"

"Miss Belder," Godfrey boomed, "you are right. Christine would have been impaled by that fetid object's horns through her head."

And Hugo said: "Quite so."

Cordelia put her arm tenderly around Christine. "Come, dear, do sit down. Let me get you something." She led Christine to the nearest chair, which was the little one in front of the spinet desk, and Christine sat down.

"I shall appreciate a lot better after this any news story about an avalanche," Christine said. "If you don't mind, Cordelia—I do think some Prunelle—"

"Of course, dear."

Cordelia went to the cellaret and took a cordial glass. She decided it was much too small for the emergency and selected a tumbler instead. She filled it with Prunelle.

A touch of nimbleness was returning to Alan's wits. He knelt by the wreckage and examined the back of the plaque, the strong wire which had held it to its supporting hook. He heard Hugo say to him: "Well?"

"The wire was worn through, Hugo." (Yes, it could have been simply that. A curious coincidence in a million that after all the years it had been hanging there—but—His fingers were suddenly careful and concealing over a slender little length of wire that seemed foreign to the others.) "It snapped."

"Well, well!"

"Hugo," Christine said, "take that thing out and bury it somewhere, will you? I never could understand why Charley ever shot it in the first place."

"Certainly, Christine."

Hugo took the boar's head and left the room, while Alan stood slowly up and, after another glance at it which explained nothing and did him no good, slipped the odd little length of wire into his jacket pocket. *Had* it been a murder trap? *Was* the Dove already in the house and the tusked boar's falling a true result of his highly perfected technique in the arts of death? Alan's head began to swim again.

What was Cordelia saying?

"The Prunelle, dear," Cordelia was saying, and handing the tumbler to Christine.

No. This was too much. Alan clutched at reason and completely missed. Prunelle, too, had been on the list. He heard his normally enchanting voice choke out: "Prunelle! Darling—wouldn't brandy—" But Christine had already swallowed some of the dubious stuff.

"You know I loathe brandy, Alan." Christine put the tumbler on the desk. It was still over half full. "There's enough in this to stock a camel."

He stood looking at her with rapt fascination, waiting for the usual manifestations. What were they? Turn cerise? White? A groan, or a shriek, or a collapse? With strychnine, of course, she would form a hoop. He pulled himself together, brushing the odd picture aside. He was kaleidoscopically aware that Hugo had rejoined them. Alan forced himself to walk normally to Christine's side and say with tender concern: "Darling, why not lie down and rest?"

Christine stood up.

"I think I will. Later we shall have some bridge."

"Lean on me, dear."

"Oh, really, Alan!"

"Why don't you go right to bed, Aunt Christine?" Lida said.

"Bed? My dear child, it is barely half-past nine, and I am chained to the habit of making at least one grand slam a night."

Christine started for the door to her suite, with Alan hovering at her elbow.

"Your grandaunt's bridge, Miss Belder," Hugo said, "is based on an effective little system originally cooked up by Captain Kidd."

Christine gave him a wicked smile. "Dear Hugo! Simply a quinine pill in reverse. The sugar is on the inside. I shall rejoin you, Lida, in an hour—carrying my letters of marque."

"I will go in and stay with you," Alan said.

Christine looked at him in amazement.

"My dear Alan, why?"

"I just want to, Christine. We could have a game of double Canfield."

Christine said to Lida that he loathed it, that usually he had to be bribed even to cut the cards. She assured Alan that she really did want to rest. She left, almost, in fact quite actually, closing the door in Alan's face.

He remained standing before it, leaving his back to the others (wasn't it Sarah Bernhardt who had once played a scene in such fashion?) while seeking, like a swimmer who has plunged too deep, to raise himself to the placid surface and the sun. He clutched, as he had always clutched when in the grip of an emotional crisis, at some accomplished role which would serve both as a precedent and a pattern for immediate behavior. Robert Montgomery? In *Night Must Fall*?

Yes, that was it: the smiling, boyish, *trustworthy* face of murder. Had Montgomery, during his hours of dread purpose, felt alone? As Alan felt alone. He caught the sardonic cynicism in Hugo's voice as Hugo said to him: "The solicitous, in fact the complete husband. You reminded me of an anxious destroyer on convoy duty." Alan turned, already boyishly trustworthy and perturbed, with a thin, fine plating of truculent manliness over it all.

"I am worried about her."

"Well, aren't we all?" Hugo's smile became insultingly cynical as he added: "Now?"

Cordelia began gathering the coffee cups and arranging them on the Sheffield tray, and Godfrey said gloomily to Lida: "Shall I tell you what Christine *really* left us for?"

"If you wish. I can understand her being very tired and nervously shocked."

"That is nonsense. Neither that boar's head falling nor the day in town could affect her nerves, which are of steel. It is dishes."

"Dishes?"

"And pots and pans. It keeps up the agreeable fiction that they are washed by magic."

"Godfrey and I," Cordelia said, "will have done them by the time dear Christine returns from her after-dinner rest. We always do."

"But you must let me help."

"No, dear, thank you. Godfrey and I are thoroughly accustomed to doing them, and it makes us feel happy—as though we were repaying in some little way Christine's great kindness to us."

"Cordelia," Godfrey said, "you will speak for yourself."

The magic of the role was working, and Alan, as secure within it as within some private tower, was in full sweep as the agreeable host. He stood beside the cellaret with his handsomely tanned fingers poised over bottles.

"Will you have some kirsch, Miss Belder?" (Should he call her Lida? After all, the competent and smooth young article, with her steady blue-green eyes, was, by marriage, his grandniece too. A beautiful flash from heaven struck him. She couldn't be Christine's heiress, because the annuity left the old witch nothing to leave. But hadn't he heard—*surely* he had heard that Lida was wealthy in her own right? The Boston obstacle, Vanbuskirk? Alan smiled.)

"There are also," he went on charmingly, "Curasao, benedictine, cognac, or a dozen other cordials if you prefer."

"I think a little kirsch, please, Mr. Admont. I've never tried it."

Alan's hovering fingers lifted the bottle of kirsch. Godfrey said: "It is made of peach pits."

"The same," Cordelia added placidly, "as prussic acid." With a galvanic shock the bottle of kirsch slipped from Alan's (again) palsied fingers and into the ice bucket. He managed to retrieve it. He thought: Good God, in another instant I'll be confessing like a fool. He searched for something immediate on which to pin his present and recent visible fits of alarm. He continued to search as Hugo said: "Is this sudden, and I might add remarkable, worry about Christine a general one, Alan? Or can you segregate it?"

Of course! That woman—Christine bête noire, who was always being shaken in their faces—would do.

"It is that woman, Hugo. The one who threatened Christine several years ago. The one she calls Laura."

"Oh, surely not," Lida said. "You can't mean that some woman actually *threatened* Aunt Christine?"

"Laura Destin," Cordelia said placidly.

"Destin?" Alan looked at Cordelia closely. "You know her last name?"

"Oh yes. One afternoon quite a while ago Christine told me all about her. We were steaming clams."

"I dare say you think Christine told you all."

"No, she was unusually factual. I think I will have a little cognac tonight, please, Alan."

Hugo regarded Cordelia with fascinated admiration. "How you manage it, Cordelia, almost approaches the clinical."

Alan, once more in stride, served cordials, and Lida said: "But what *is* this about this woman, Miss Banning?"

"Laura Destin was staying here as a friend, just as I am. Just as all of us are. Christine said Miss Destin did do the loveliest sewing. She had only been here for a week or two, but even so she evidently had come to consider the arrangement as a permanent one."

"If Belder Tor had a theme song," Godfrey boomed at Lida, "it would be called the 'Song of the Leech.'"

"I'm just beginning to realize you don't mean a thing that you say, Mr. Lance."

"The child is not only fey, she drips with dew."

"Well, anyhow," Cordelia plugged placidly on, "before she came here Laura Destin had disposed of her sole piece of property, a farm up in Maine. She said at a loss. Then when she was downright mean to Christine, Christine just asked her to go."

"I should like to know what form the meanness took," Hugo said.

"She refused to hemstitch a dozen little towels."

"Revolt!" Godfrey boomed delightedly.

"No, Miss Destin just turned horrid. She accused Christine of casting her adrift into a heartless world where she had neither relatives nor friends nor a pillow to rest her head."

"Cordelia, that is straight out of *East Lynne*."

"I can't help it, Godfrey. It's what Christine told me. Miss Destin did leave Belder Tor, of course, but she told Christine that she would come back and that Christine would be sorry for what she had done. She went so far as to threaten revenge. I understand that Miss Destin was Scottish. She put a malediction upon Christine in pure Erse."

"Impossible. The language is devoid of vowels."

Hugo smiled cynically at Alan and said: "But doesn't all this come under the heading of Ancient History?"

"No, it doesn't." (This Destin angle was working out far better than Alan had dared to hope. Surely some icing, some embellishment could be added to make it even more palatable still?) "Christine mentioned the woman to me only this morning before she drove to town. I had the definite impression that Laura Destin had tried to get in touch with her." He turned gallantly to Lida. "I hope this doesn't alarm you too greatly? It's mostly conjecture, but naturally I'm concerned."

"I should think you would be. Why on earth doesn't Aunt Christine report the woman to the police?"

"Christine," Hugo said, "is a remarkable person, Miss Belder. She prefers to remain a force sufficient unto itself. Personally, Alan, I think your worries are rubbish. If Christine truly had received a letter she would never have stopped this side of Duse in capitalizing on it. No, the Destin woman was a worthless stray, and is probably either dead or in the poorhouse." Hugo started to leave the room. He said, just before he went through the door, "I shall be busy in the laboratory until Christine descends upon us for bridge—in a poor attempt at catching up on the day's wasted time."

Godfrey picked up the Sheffield tray.

"Are you ready for the pearl diving, Cordelia? Shall we get on with our own slight task of love?"

"Won't you please let me help you, Miss Banning?" Lida asked.

"Absolutely not, dear, but it is sweet of you to want to." She followed Godfrey out of the room, and Alan watched them go while satisfaction mounted warmly in him at a fence that had been so competently, so artistically hurdled. His look turned to Lida, who was already increasing rapidly in value as a potential life line to save him from dark seas and along which he could conceivably drag himself back to a comparatively golden shore.

He realized with satisfaction that they were alone.

CHAPTER IX

Lida was anything but pleased in being faced with what obviously was the brink of a tête-à-tête with Alan. She did not actively dislike him. She simply did not consider him, except in the most impersonal fashion, as an adjunct of Christine's. She would nevertheless most willingly have exchanged his present proximity for the suds session with Cordelia and Godfrey.

She observed, from the cool detachment of her eighteen years (plus the added distinguishment of a woman who has just become, officially, engaged and has marriage practically staring her in the face), the mannered gesture with which Alan opened a platinum cigarette case and offered her a cigarette.

The star-sapphire ring on his near-by finger, as he then offered her a light, fascinated her. It almost floored her. Lida's excellent eyes (20:20) took in each detail of the lion-pawed setting and the tiny claws.

She said with incontrovertible truth: "I've never seen a ring just like that before. Aren't they lion paws?"

"Yes." Alan exhibited the jewel with a handsome gesture. "It isn't bad. I saw it in one of the better shops, and Christine gave it to me for Easter."

Lida did her best.

"She—she *is* awfully kind."

"It was stupid of me to have alarmed you about her and Laura Destin."

"It would seem to be Aunt Christine who needs the alarming."

"I know, but, as Hugo indicated, she is a woman without fear. Adamant." Alan gazed charmingly at Lida and thought: A good, cold cucumber if there ever was one. Well, he'd warm her up. He lapsed suddenly into an attractive, boyish bluntness: "Look here, Lida, you must have wondered about us, didn't you? This May-and-September marriage sort of thing?"

"Why, no, of course I didn't."

"And of course you did. How much did Christine write you? About herself and myself, I mean?"

"Simply that she had decided—I mean that she and *you* had decided to get married. My principal knowledge of the wedding came from the newspaper accounts."

"Good lord, what a shock it must have been!"

"Well, it was. A little. Of course it wasn't as though Aunt Christine and I had ever been truly close."

"How like Christine to do a thing like that!" The ham in Alan ripened, and he pulled out several of his best stops. "Strange the tricks which life can play! Or should one say Fate? You yourself admit that you do not know Christine—not as she *really* is—whereas I, and I think I can say this in due modesty, I had a prescience about her from the instant we met. Have you ever felt like that about a person?"

"Oh yes—why, the first time I saw Barry I—"

"Exactly!" Alan said, snatching back the scene. "Lida, I took one look at Christine and said: Here is one of the great tragic figures of our time—a splendid woman, old, childless, widowed, and with her special temperament. What, I asked myself, was there left for her in life?"

"Why, Aunt Christine had lots of things to live for, Mr. Admont."

"Oh, my dear child! And *do* call me Alan. Christine had nothing. *Nothing* beyond the meretricious power to manufacture what golden dross she could from her lingering hours." Alan brushed all that away with a rueful gesture. "We met. I, in my poor fashion, as tragic a figure as herself. Traduced by the critics from the profession which was to have been my life. Rejected from serving my country by a weakened heart."

"You do have my sympathies in that, Mr. Admont."

"Alan."

"All right. Alan."

"But Christine, too, had her cross. Why wasn't the perfect solution that we bear it together?"

"Cross?" Lida said incredulously. "Aunt Christine?"

"Our mutual loneliness—our empty lives. She looks upon me as the son she never had, and I on her as a dear, dear friend. The marriage? It has no significance other than that she wished me to inherit her money." (Better play this safe.) "I can say so to you without offense because you have a fortune of your own. You *do* have a fortune of your own?"

"Yes, but I don't see why, if Aunt Christine wanted you to inherit her money, she took out this annuity—Oh dear, why do I say things like that?"

Alan returned to earth with a bang. "Bilked!" The word was a scream of rage.

"*Oh!*"

He grabbed at recovery and said swiftly, earnestly: "Not I—do not misunderstand me, Lida. It is Christine who has been bilked—hoodwinked by that putrid alligator who calls himself a lawyer—thwarted out of her true wishes by his miserable cajolery and bag of tricks."

The force of Alan's "Bilked!" had sent Lida into retreat, one which carried her over to the spinet desk. Alan followed her swiftly and, again within range, began battering her with his charms.

"But enough of me," he said, not without a struggle. "Tell me about yourself. Give me the true you."

Lida, in mild desperation, picked up a silver frame from the desk.

"Has Aunt Christine ever done any acting?"

"No. Not professionally."

"I thought, from this costume she's wearing, she might have."

"Costume?" For an instant Alan didn't get it. Then the blockbuster struck home. The heady wine of dreams which had charged him following Joe's departure in the morning had completely driven from his mind the empty frame from which Joe had taken Christine's portrait to give to the Dove. "You *did* say costume?"

"Yes. What a pity the photograph was folded. The crease shows right across her throat."

The Dove.

None but the Dove could have replaced that picture, could have done it during the hour while all of them were in the dining room downing Godfrey's pheasant. So he *was* here. Sweat broke into beads on Alan's noble brow. The portrait was tangible proof that the Dove was here in the house, and now. And that falling boar's head *had* been the Dove's first device. The ultimate rags of hope shredded further and fled. For a moment of darkness Alan nose-dived into chaos.

"Are you ill?" Lida said.

"You must forgive me, but I am more worried than I care to admit."

Alan opened the desk drawer and took out a long, powerful flashlight.

"Is it about Laura Destin?" Lida asked.

"Yes." (Why didn't the silly little fool shut up? Stop nagging him with her squeakings?) "I am psychic. You must accept it as a fact. I am filled with a premonition that in some fashion she has filtered into the house. Forgive my desertion, but I feel compelled to make an immediate search for him."

"Him?"

"Her!"

Alan turned and fled up the turret stairs.

CHAPTER X

Lida put the silver frame back on the spinet desk. She was beginning to wonder whether Barry hadn't after all had something on the ball when he had been dubious about Belder Tor being a seasonable place to pass a night in. Her practical mind rejected the thought as silly.

Still there had been a strangling quality about Alan's voice just now, and his exit up the stairs *had* been in the nature of a restrained track star waiting for the gun. It must have been the portrait of Christine which had caused the spasm.

Why?

Although practically on the brink of entering the younger-matron set, Lida still lacked the accolade of its poise, its self-sufficiency when alone in strange places.

And heaven knew that Belder Tor was strange, no matter how determined she was to look upon it objectively as the home of a great, if somewhat unstable, aunt.

What was more, she *felt* alone. It was all right to say that Christine was near by in her suite, that Godfrey and Cordelia were potting and panning in the kitchen, while Alan, plus flashlight, was probing the empty upper regions of the dismal pile for a fugitive from *East Lynne*; the fact remained that for all the good they did her they just weren't.

It would be nice to call up Barry, but he probably hadn't reached the Plaza as yet, and even if he had, what would she say? I must tell you, darling, that a fog is pressing with wraithlike fingers against the windows? That mine host is hot after a vengeful woman who threatened Christine in Erse? And how, dear, are the aunts? What dismal bilge!

A look told Lida that so far as the fog was concerned her thoughts were correct: the panes of the windows and french doors were a beady black. That is, except for one of the doors, and that one distinctly showed, pressed against its glass, a woman's face. Oh, she thought, that good old pressing face! Never mind. Bromidic as the chill-stirrer was, the face was there, and Lida's sturdy, well-controlled heart did a flip.

The face had evidently decided not to act true to form: it did not vanish, with the almost obligatory background music of a shriek from Lida and, when all would rush out, an empty terrace. No. Its eyes stared right back at her, and then, without further ado or spine-icing trappings, the woman opened the french door and stepped into the room.

Lida noted that the woman's furs and style were in the rating of super-elegant, that the knitted head scarf loosely knotted at the throat and the gloves and leather handbag were a violent cerise, that the face was handsome and hard and the general manner was nervous. This, Lida decided at once, is Laura Destin.

"Is this Belder Tor?" the woman said.

"But you *know* it is."

"Listen, dear, in this pogo field for zombies anything could be anything. I tried the front door, but nothing happened. I pushed every knob I could find that might have been a bell and then walked around the house and saw you. I want to see Mrs. Admont."

"Then you aren't Laura Destin?"

"I'm not. No matter who she is. My name is—well, never mind what it is. Just tell Mrs. Admont I want to see her."

"She's resting."

The woman seemed nervously tired. She sank into an armchair. She said: "Look, dearie, you go and tell her that this is important. It's important to *her*."

It is important, Lida thought, that Christine be warned immediately that Laura Destin was in the house. Not for a moment did Lida decide to swallow that never-mind-what-my-name-is stuff.

"I'll let her know."

Belle Crystal watched Lida open the door to Christine's suite and disappear. Now that the step had been taken, Belle wasn't quite so sure. It had seemed a good idea in the morning while Belle had been listening to Joe talking with Alan on the telephone. It had seemed the only idea. Then.

Belle had known for some time that Joe was nearing the point where he'd wash her up, an operation that had always been perfectly final with her predecessors. Joe, when Belle came right down to it, was a simple soul. His range included none but the primary colors in life. And in death.

Belle shivered beneath her costly summer furs. There was nothing to lose, when you came right down to it. Sell her information and conjectures to Christine Admont as to the mess which Joe and Alan were unquestionably boiling, sell it for whatever she could, and then beat it. Beat it like hell.

She opened the cerise handbag and took out a mirror. Her lips could stand a repaint where she had been biting them. She got out the lipstick and went to work. Her back was partially toward the doorway leading to the dining room, kitchen, and lower general rooms of the wing. It was partly reflected, this doorway, in the little mirror, and (Belle started suddenly) there was someone, or something, standing very quietly out in the dim shadows of the hallway.

Was it?

Belle's gloved fingers trembled.

She forced herself to go on with the job on her lips.

CHAPTER XI

The morning room was empty when, about ten minutes later, Christine came into it with Lida. The french door which Belle Crystal had used stood ajar. The corridor door was closed. Fog sifted thinly in from the terrace and the dark, quiet night.

"But she's gone," Lida said.

"Yes. I remember her as having been strange."

"Do let me get Mr. Admont, Aunt Christine."

"But he's already looking, dear, you said."

"Not outside. And that terrace door is open. She closed it after she came in."

Christine shrugged.

"My dear, you couldn't find a haystack here at night, much less a needle. But get him if it will make you feel any better."

Christine finished buckling the belt to the velvet house dress she had been putting on. She watched Lida run up the turret stairs. She found herself standing near the spinet desk, with the half-emptied glass of Prunelle still on its surface, where she had left it. She picked it up.

She was about to finish the Prunelle when her eyes concentrated on the open french door. Her hand hesitated in mid-air and she returned the glass to the desk. She went over and opened the french door further. She called into the darkness of the night and the limpid fog: "Laura? Are you out here, Laura?"

It was very queer. Lida's description of the woman could have applied to Laura Destin, but Christine felt oddly that it did not. There was a flamboyancy about the summer furs and brilliant accessories which engendered doubt. Laura had been a rockish, all-but-drab creature. But there had been a certain flair. Could it have come to fruition during the few brief years?

Christine came back from the terrace. For a moment she speculated about the closed corridor door. The fog, the stillness, there was nothing she could attribute it to, but she felt very strongly that someone was standing on the other side of the door. Laura? Possibly. Swiftly she opened the door. For no reason on earth that she could determine, it shocked her strongly to find Hugo facing her.

"Hugo—you startled me!"

"Sorry, Christine."

Hugo came in and closed the door. He took a deliberate stand against it, blocking it almost defensively. "Did you see her?" Christine said. "Is she out there?" Hugo studied Christine's unnatural pallor, the dilated pupils of her violet eyes.

"See who, Christine?"

"Laura Destin. She came in from the terrace while Lida was in here alone. Lida came in and told me."

"And you found Laura—gone?"

"Yes. I was lying down and simply took time to throw on this rag. The room was empty, but that terrace door was open. What on earth do you make of it?"

"Obviously the woman is deranged, and even I can not tell what goes on in the mind of a neurotic. Did Miss Belder come back in here with you?"

"Yes."

"Where is she now?"

"She went upstairs to look for Alan."

"Then you have been in here alone, Christine?"

"Yes. Hugo, it worries me."

"May I suggest that you do not worry too much? I am your friend, Christine. All of us are your friends. Everything will turn out all right."

"You say that so significantly."

"The more strongly to impress you with my sincerity."

"You certainly are developing a sibyl touch, Hugo."

Lida came running down the turret stairs and joined them. She was in somewhat of a state of nerves. "I can't find him, Aunt Christine. I'll admit that when I reached the dark stairs to the top floor I just said no!"

"Lida, you're trembling," Christine said, putting an arm around her. "I used to too. For the first seventeen years we lived here."

"I'm all right now."

"Were you upstairs long?" Hugo asked.

"A lifetime, Doctor."

There was something in Hugo's attitude that Lida could not gauge: his eyes were shadowed with a private knowledge which he had no intention whatever, she felt, of sharing with them. It was more than the dark and emptiness of the upper floor which had upset her; it was the completely casual manner with which Christine had accepted Laura Destin's arrival and presumed departure. It was all right to be eccentric and nicely mad if you didn't carry it too *far*.

She felt Christine's arm press more closely about her, and it was almost as though she were being propelled to the door to Christine's suite.

"Come with me," Christine said. "We will smother your nerves with a monologue on your part about each attractive facet of Barry. We will forget Laura. She is gone."

"It will be bridge as usual, Christine," Hugo said. "Am I right?"

"Hugo, you remain monotonously right."

Hugo permitted himself one leisurely smile at the shut door. He turned, and his eyes were speculative on the jog in the wall beside the turret stairs. How far, he wondered, would the others follow along the path which with utter callousness he had so instantly mapped? The full length of it, if he knew them. And he did.

There were only so many worlds which each of them could build, including himself, as warm refuges for their warped and almost clinically selfish lives. No, no matter at what an extravagance of sophistry must this one be permitted to crash down upon their heads.

Hugo did not hurry, and still he wasted no time. His movements suggested the trained precision of a surgeon as he went to the small door of the quick-freezer locker by the turret stairs and opened it.

He reached inside and switched on a light. Stretching along the right wall of this cubicle was a sheeting of silvered metal glazed with light frost. The facing wall was fronted by a rack from which hung Christine's fur coats and capes and scarfs.

Hugo left the door standing open. He went unhurriedly out into the corridor and, after a very brief while, came back into the room carrying, almost cradled in his arms, Belle Crystal's corpse.

CHAPTER XII

Hugo went to the cellaret and mixed himself a stiff drink of scotch. He could hear Godfrey's voice booming louder out in the corridor in one of his interminable reminiscences of meals' from Godfrey's Lucullan past.

"—then after the roulade of sand dabs they sprang a Scotch grouse *rôti nature* that was a lulu. Naturally, Cordelia, the meal ended with *petit cœur à la crème aux frais rafraîchies.*"

They came in then, and Cordelia said: "It sounds awfully nice, Godfrey, I'm sure."

She went to the spinet desk and started taking playing cards, pencils and score pads from a drawer while Godfrey joined Hugo at the cellaret.

Hugo asked him: "Has Alan been back in the kitchen with you, Godfrey?"

"Do not be stupid. It is beneath that egocentric vulture's imaginary birthright even to enter a kitchen. Why?"

"I am interested in where various people recently were."

The tumbler on the spinet desk, with its still unfinished portion of Christine's private Prunelle, fascinated Cordelia. She could not resist lifting the glass and sniffing its aroma. Her sense of smell was as keenly trained as her sense of touch, and although she had only once (months ago) tasted the liqueur, its aroma now seemed infinitesimally different—scarcely a shade, but still there was a difference.

Absently she heard Hugo saying to Godfrey: "Have you and Cordelia been together in the kitchen since you went out of here?"

And Godfrey replying testily: "Is this a Gestapo spelling bee you are instituting, Hugo?"

Cordelia carried the glass to her lips. She was about to drink its contents when Hugo said to her sharply: "Cordelia!" She started and jerked the glass down. It struck the desk's rim and fell to the floor, where the Prunelle emptied slowly out onto the rug.

"Oh *dear!*" Cordelia picked up the empty glass and went to the cellaret for a bar cloth to mop up the rug.

Hugo's voice grew sterner: "Listen to me, Cordelia. Was Godfrey with you in the kitchen all of the time you were doing the dishes?"

Godfrey's voice was virtuous. "Not once were these precious fingers devoid of suds from that rancid sink."

"Yes, Hugo," Cordelia said, "Godfrey was with me all of the time—except when he carried the things into the butler's pantry and put them away."

"How long did that take him?"

"Answer, Cordelia," Godfrey said. "Herr Himmler himself is speaking to you."

A french door opened, and Alan walked in from the terrace. He heard Cordelia say: "I haven't the remotest idea, Hugo." He headed directly for the cellaret and poured himself a drink.

"Witch-hunting again, I suppose?" Hugo said to him.

"No, I wasn't witch-hunting. And stop picking on me, Hugo. I'm upset."

Cordelia put cards on the bridge table. "I wonder if he's upset about the annuity?" she said to Godfrey.

Alan's nerves were completely on edge. "I am upset from just having looked this rat-infested warren over, as well as the grounds, for Laura Destin."

"And did you see her?" Hugo asked.

"No."

"Miss Belder did. It would seem that Miss Belder was alone in here when Miss Destin walked in from the terrace to pay a little call on Christine."

"Oh dear. Oh *dear!*" Cordelia said, sinking weakly onto one of the small chairs at the bridge table. "Godfrey—a small glass of sherry, please, or, if you insist, some scotch."

Alan's handsome face was paper white. He said nothing while Hugo told them Christine's story—her version, Hugo called it, of the woman's eccentric arrival and apparent departure.

"Then Christine is all right?" Alan said in a curiously calm voice.

"In a physical sense," Hugo said, "yes. Lida is in with her, glutting the air with rhapsodies about her unique young man."

"What do you mean—in a physical sense?"

Hugo finished his drink. He contemplatively observed Godfrey's great hulk deep in a comfortable armchair. He studied Cordelia's soft plumpness in the little chair, with the highball she held so lovingly in her dimpled hand. He was complacently interested in the trace of sweat which beaded Alan's brow. Yes, Hugo decided, they were ripe enough for it now.

"Before I answer that," he said to Alan, "I am wondering just how far the three of you would go to protect your futures."

Godfrey set down his empty glass.

"What are you getting at, Hugo?"

"The question seems perfectly plain. You, Godfrey, are forty something, and you, Cordelia, are in your fifties." Hugo's tone took on an unpleasant bite. "Your comparative youth, Alan, does not exclude you from the general premises. What would happen to each of us—for I include myself—if we were forced to leave here?" Cordelia's scotch-hazy eyes were suddenly bleak.

"I don't know, Hugo."

Hugo lighted a cigarette while permitting the thought to sink in.

I really *don't* know what I would do, Cordelia was thinking, if it weren't for Christine and Belder Tor. Hugo was perfectly right about her age. As a matter of fact, she would be sixty-one next March. She thought of her comfort here, her little amusements, of the shelter which Christine's name and position gave to her occasional forays upon the stores. Of all the good food and warmth and of her lovely bed—so soft—like sleeping on a cloud.

Two fat tears shaped and trembled in her eyes. The scotch, added to her nips and Number Thirties, had made her more than usually mellow. She had felt so rosy until—what was it? Oh yes, until Hugo had started to ask his sad questions. How desolate the friendly room had become. From the cluttered storehouse of Cordelia's memory arose that heartbreaking poem which had driven her in her far-off childhood so satisfyingly into tears.

"Curfew," she said quietly, "shall not ring tonight."

They ignored her, except for Hugo, who smiled sardonically and refilled her glass with scotch.

Godfrey was thinking of his comfort too. But it was more than that. Incredibly, he was still complacent of his genius even after the fiasco at the Lewis Galleries last spring. He was determined to make his mark. Never had he doubted his ability to do so except during those moments in the past when downright hunger had weakened him, and as long as Belder Tor sheltered him he would not be without food.

Godfrey was further convinced that the world was not ready for him as yet. But when the boys came home he foresaw a future of a United States gone suddenly Continental. Never before had so many gone abroad to such far-flung corners of the earth. And a complete cross section of the country had gone.

The money had always been here, and soon, with their new and globally nourished good taste, the returning generation would be his plum. The fighting, the war *in ipso*, had never registered with Godfrey in the slightest, and he viewed the world-shaking struggle solely in such terms as reflected his own special advantages.

"I think I would go pretty far, Hugo," he said.

Hugo turned to Alan.

"You, Alan, I do not have to ask. Your status has done a complete somersault since Christine sank your golden future into an annuity. You are now in the boat with the rest of us. If anything happens to Christine, you, too, are sunk."

"Nothing will happen to her. I'll see to that."

"Physically, perhaps. But can you protect her mind?"

"You are right, Hugo," Godfrey said gloomily. "Of course she must be crazy, or she never would put up with us."

"No, Hugo," Cordelia said. "She is just refreshingly original."

"And I tell you that she may already have slipped over the border line and have suffered a mental lapse. Possibly the proper place right now for Christine would be a sanitarium."

"What good would she do us in a sanitarium?" Godfrey asked.

"Precisely."

Alan was belligerent. "What are you trying to do? Have her put away? I won't stand for this kind of talk, Hugo."

Hugo ignored him. "Would you," he asked all of them, "connive at covering up a murder?"

Alan's face lost its last trace of color. His handsome eyes flashed stealthily toward the portrait of Christine on the spinet desk, with its chilling reminder of the presence of the Dove in the house. He did his best to lower the familiar curtain which would shut out whatever deadly thing it might be which Hugo must have hit upon and plainly intended to divulge, but the curtain would not fall.

In spite of this panic which seized him, Alan still could not resist savoring the drama of the situation with its content of sheer theater. What was that play? It didn't matter: there must have been clusters of them, each with its essential scene when the conspirators were bonded into unity by their evil and common intent.

Only the setting was new. No deserted heath, this room, and definitely not a Moscow cellar during the last days of the czars. But the cast was true to form. Alan's eyes (now stage-directorial) observed them professionally: the brooding mood, each deep in the slough of his selfish desires, and with it all the beading, wistful fog against the night's dark panes.

It was a dream which he had dreamed before. It had been dreamed this morning between himself and Joe, only now it was Cordelia and Godfrey who were weighing in the balance the danger to themselves against the advantage. Cordelia, Alan realized, was too filled with scotch to do anything but float like a soft and translucent jellyfish wherever Hugo's current might dictate.

Godfrey would make his own decision, but it was a foregone conclusion: nothing, no venture, however perilous, would advise him to pull up the roots which he had sunk into Belder Tor.

And of Hugo himself? Fear spread in shallow waves of ice through Alan. *What did Hugo know?*

"Don't you think you are stretching this to the breaking point?" Alan asked.

"Christine has killed that woman," Hugo said.

CHAPTER XIII

Cordelia spilled scotch on her velvet dress.

"You say it so coldly, Hugo," she sighed.

"Coldly? Why not?" Hugo gave an irritated shrug. "What was the Destin woman to me?" (This was, of course, true. No death would ever have the slightest meaning for Hugo, except his own.) "It is Christine alone who must matter to all of us."

Godfrey felt a stab of sharp anguish. Here indeed was an enemy powerful enough to shatter his dreams. His sense of security fled before the bitter gale of Hugo's grim convictions. He tried desperately to keep his voice from shaking.

"What drove her into this stupidity? What made her do it?"

"Does it matter?" Hugo asked impatiently. "Surely we know her well enough to appreciate that she will never tell us. She will never admit for an instant to being the author of this crime. I assure you as a doctor, as a man who has made a profound study of just such mental conditions, that Christine is an utterly conscienceless woman of steel."

"She is the Borgia type," Godfrey agreed gloomily. "The Catherine of Russia."

"It is simple for me to vision her alone in here after Lida Belder went upstairs. Christine looks for Laura. She looks out in the hallway. She sees Laura's shadowy figure entering that empty room next to the laboratory. Christine follows, then she faces that woman whom she had once thrown out of Belder Tor and who had had the temerity, the audacity, to threaten her."

Cordelia's voice floated blurredly through the silence. "Surely she must have threatened dear Christine again. Perhaps with a gun. And then Christine caused her to 'pass away' in order to save her own life."

"And I tell you," Hugo insisted, "that we will never know the actual details. You may be right, Cordelia, and I think you are. We must conspire to keep the same silence which I can assure you Christine will keep. Her story will remain unshaken: she came in with Lida Belder, and the woman was no longer here. The incident for Christine is finished."

"It's all very well for you to say that the incident is finished," Godfrey said, with a desperate stab at the practical, "but how about the body? Where is it, Hugo?"

"It *was* in the room next to the laboratory. I think the room was formerly used as the servants' hall. I heard a noise in there while I was working, like a chair overturning. As though somebody had stumbled against one in the dark. When I had finished what I was doing I went into the room to see."

Alan feverishly wiped his brow.

"Are you sure she was dead?"

Hugo looked at Alan pityingly.

"Do not be stupid. I am accustomed to cadavers. I do not know what weapon Christine used, but a blow on the head did the trick."

"Christine's mind," Cordelia said, "must have been a perfect blank."

Hugo paused while they absorbed the picture. "Well?" he said finally. "Do you want me to call the police? Shall each of our lives be microscopically examined under the light of a murder investigation, in addition to our meal ticket being sent to the chair? All to the stupid purpose that a futile justice be done that lone woman? We can assume that she has no relatives or friends beyond those of the most casual nature, and that no one other than her own crazed self knew of her visit here. I am confident her loss will instigate no inquiry. Are we, for such a tramp, to be uprooted and thrown out to combat the bitter world with our wretchedly minuscule resources?"

"But after all," Godfrey insisted in a shaken whisper, "there *is* the woman's body."

"That does not trouble me."

"The lake," Cordelia moaned. "The gentle and concealing waters."

"Of course!" Alan said sharply. "The lake. Just off the point where Christine has those damn picnics. There's a good ninety-foot depth."

"No," Hugo said decisively. "Bodies rise, not matter how securely they may seem to be anchored. I tell you not to worry about it. I carried it from that room and put it in the quick freezer, where it will keep cold until I arrange for its permanent disposal."

"But won't dear Christine miss it?" Cordelia asked. "I mean if she goes back to look for it and finds it gone?"

"She will rationalize that fact as easily as she rationalized the deed itself. Christine will simply decide that the blow she struck had not been fatal. She will be satisfied that Laura Destin recovered from it and, in panic, fled."

"Fled on what?" Godfrey asked.

"In her car, naturally. How do you suppose she got here? It is a small coupe. I found it parked on the drive and have already put it in the garage with the others for the night."

"I cannot help but think," Cordelia announced with sudden precision, "that this time Christine has overstepped."

Godfrey said, "My God!" and added: "Let us hope that it doesn't become a habit with her."

"More so than ever now, we must be *very* kind to her."

Alan said abruptly: "I don't like the idea of that body being in the freezer. Can't you get rid of it tonight, Hugo?"

"I think you are right. I shall attend to it after everyone is asleep."

"You are certain that the murderer—was—Christine?"

Hugo gave Alan and Cordelia and Godfrey a pregnant look.

"Isn't it advisable to let the matter rest on that assumption? For all of us?" he said.

How clever, Cordelia thought, dear Hugo is! There was so rarely any circumlocution about him: he would strike to the heart of a problem, the *true* heart, and make it so simple to understand. And in this one the heart was Christine. Through a slight haze (again rosy) Cordelia saw Christine coming into the room with Lida. Christine simply did not look like a murderess. Cordelia's eyes passed fondly over Hugo and Godfrey and Alan. No, she decided, none of them does. She sighed reluctantly and thought: Too bad that one of them is.

"Alan," Christine said, "I've just promised Lida that tomorrow we will have a picnic luncheon by the lake. I want her to enjoy the few moments she wall be here with us."

"Did you see any sign of Laura Destin?" Lida asked Alan.

"No."

"Miss Belder," Hugo said incisively, "let us simply forget about it. The woman suffered one of her aberrations and came to call on Christine. That is all."

"And took herself away again," Cordelia added helpfully. "For good."

They settled themselves for bridge. Cordelia wisely announced that she would simply sit and watch the game, and Alan cut out. He was magnetized to the cellaret, where he mixed himself a stiff drink. Could he, he asked himself dispassionately, stand all this? Was it *good* for him? He looked in a Venetian mirror paneled on the wall. Haggard, yes, but the old stuff was still there, still capable of doing its tricks. Sanity presented, as a sole solution to safety, the imperative need of getting Christine to flee with him.

As to the leverage to use to induce her into flight, it was stupid of him not to have hit upon the solution before: He could dangle Hollywood, with its glittering bedizenments, as a bait. God knew, he thought bitterly, that Hollywood would amuse the old wreck.

The fact that his theatrical career had been interred with a full embalming job in *Jupiter Returns* did not matter. Not now, when the studios were grabbing everyone left by the draft who could still move onto a set without a wheel chair. Publicity—a career—his features flashed before swooning (female) millions—before Joe.

No.

No, that was out, because Joe was tireless and would never rest. All that was left him in this contrary, this wickedly thankless world was a flight in solo. But on what? Alan took another deep pull on the drink, and his thoughts slid brilliantly into groove: how fatuous that the idea hadn't struck him a thousand times before now! Christine's jewels. Yes, he would steal the jewels and be off. And never come back.

Mexico?

Warming into pleasanter reality with each stiff swallow waxed a Mexican dream. It evolved in cinematic structure, with himself a velvet-trousered caballero luxuriously installed in a hacienda, thanks to Christine's jewels.

Sold one by one, they would surely last until he had roped in a rich senora in her dotage, complete with either a silver mine or oil wells. Yes, he would do it. Let Christine (no longer precious, nor an albatross) face her fate with the Dove as best she might. Let Joe cool off in his own good time. He felt excitingly free and at his most alluring by the time he had finished the drink. He was, in fact, again his good old self. But that surface would never do. He assumed a frown of truculent, boyish worry when the rubber over at the bridge table was done.

"Christine," he said, "I have been thinking. That woman may have had robbery in mind."

Christine looked up from the score pad.

"Quite possibly. I always felt she was a thief."

"She might return. Get me your jewels, and I will put them in the safe for the night."

Alan saw the narrowing of Hugo's eyes and the swift belligerence that came over Godfrey's broad face. Inwardly he smiled. Okay, punks, he thought, think what you like, for there is nothing you can do: there's a stiff in that freezer, and none of you can open his trap.

Christine stood up and left the room.

"That's a good idea," Lida said.

Idly Alan wondered whether Lida might have any trinkets of worth with which to swell the loot. He imagined not, not with her here, unless it were the diamond clip which Cordelia, awash with scotch, had given her.

Hugo said softly: "I wondered when you'd get around to that, old man."

Alan went right on riding the crest. "Do not," he said truculently to Hugo, "call me old man." Then Christine was back in the room. Her jewel case wasn't with her. She carried instead a tagged key.

"But the jewels, dear?" Alan said.

Christine's brittle little laugh gave Alan a chill. Too frequently in his experience with her had similar small laughs been the prelude to some deviltry of a truly fiendish sort.

"Dear," she said, "I shall save you from worrying through a sleepless night. Several years ago I had my collection copied in excellent paste. The genuine stones are in a vault in New York. If Laura did plan to come back and steal them, all she would get would be glass."

"They look so real, Aunt Christine," Lida said, while thinking that never had a man possessed so many hues, for Alan's stunning face was shifting chromatically from an oyster gray to the color of eggplant.

"Yes," Christine said, "it was a good job. My furs, however, are a different matter. I store them here during the summer, Lida, in our quick freezer. It's never kept locked, but tonight it would be wiser."

"Oh *dear*!" wailed Cordelia.

Alan all but strangled out: "Your furs, Christine?"

"Alan, *stop* standing there like a Stoughton bottle. As I remember it, Laura used to be hypnotically fascinated with my sables."

Christine walked over to the freezer door.

"Let me, dear!" Alan cried, jumping after her. "Give me the key, dear!"

"Alan, isn't this solicitude more than usually thick? I wonder whether it will turn cold tomorrow."

Alan's teeth were almost chattering.

"Cold?"

Christine put a hand on the freezer doorknob. "Perhaps a beaver jacket for the picnic—it takes so long to get the chill out when they've been hanging in here. Have you any warm things, Lida?"

"Yes, I've a sweater, Aunt Christine."

"Tomorrow," Godfrey boomed, "will be hot as blazes, Christine."

"I rather think you are right."

Christine locked the freezer door.

"Do let me take care of the key, dear?"

Alan implored. Christine slipped the key into the house-gown pocket. "Alan, I will not be treated as though *both* of my feet were in the grave."

It was all too much. With one tragic cry of "Grave!" Alan crumpled and fell flat on his face.

"He's fainted," Cordelia announced placidly, "and I really think it will do him good."

CHAPTER XIV

Day broke on a rancid sky, and by eleven o'clock the morning had developed into a horror: gray, damp, and chill. The morning room was depressing beyond words and presented, in a cold, somber light, all the slight traces of disorder from the night before.

Godfrey was clearing up. His thoughts were bleak, and it deeply offended his sense of the fitness of things on observing Lida as she ran happily down the turret stairs and came into the room. She looked abominably wholesome and rested, in an almost schoolgirl skirt and blouse.

She said with what Godfrey considered perfectly putrid brightness: "Good morning, Mr. Lance."

Godfrey looked at his watch. He looked at her hideously bright smile.

"It is almost eleven o'clock," he said. "You shall have no breakfast."

"Such a lovely rest!" Lida's smile deepened. "And I bet everybody else is in bed, too."

"You are wrong."

"Is Miss Banning down?"

"Cordelia left here early with Hugo to get some things for this disgusting picnic we are to be compelled to suffer."

"Well, I'll see her when they get back."

Godfrey stopped gathering up score pads and looked at Lida sharply. What did this bursting moppet know? Had she got on to something? Cordelia so truly was the one weak link in the chain which bound her and himself and Alan and Hugo in the fetters of their uncomfortable secret.

"What do you want to see Cordelia about?"

"I want to return the diamond clip she gave me. I feel sure it was nothing but an impulsive gesture on her part. I just know that it must be an heirloom."

"It hasn't had time."

"Well, I feel she must cherish it, and I don't feel right about keeping it."

"You are a sensible girl. Return the clip. Before," Godfrey added darkly, "its heat burns you."

"I've left it out on my bureau so I won't forget. Has Mr. Admont recovered from his attack of nerves? Is he all right this morning?"

"Alan is changing his clothes. The silly fool sat up all night on a chair before Christine's door. I think he is mad. He remains obsessed with the fixed idea that something desperate may happen to her. I reject the old anecdote about a saber-toothed tiger."

"Is she up?"

"What folly! Christine is having her breakfast in bed. We make a pool every morning as to which of her stock excuses she will use for doing so. Care to get in on it?"

"Not today, thank you." Lida smiled and looked through a window at the dreary sky. "It's pretty stormy-looking, isn't it? Do you suppose the picnic will be called off?"

"No. When Christine decides on a thing it is done. As a result, as soon as Cordelia and Hugo get back we will spread ourselves out on moist rocks beneath a canopy of dripping trees and not only enjoy ourselves but damn well better had."

"I like picnics."

"I am convinced that you do."

"Where will we have it?"

"There is an execrable open fireplace built on the shore of the lake at about a five-minute walk from here. On that primitive and repulsive arrangement I am supposed to broil chickens and roast ears of corn. The prospect embraces all the grotesque horror of an Albrecht Durer print."

"Well, it sounds pretty elegant right now."

"Do not look upon me as such a beast."

"But I'm not!"

"You are. A ravenous young beast. I shall get you some coffee and one piece of toast as soon as I finish clearing up."

"Then this time you can't stop me from helping you." Lida began to plump chair cushions, while Godfrey put the bridge table away and started rearranging chairs.

He said: "After this malodorous imitation of a *fête champêtre de grand luxe* is over with, I shall start your portrait. I have changed my mind. I shall not do your flesh in lettuce green. I shall do it in cerulean blue. Behind you will be dolls and asphodels."

Lida had reached, in her plumping, the armchair where she had left the mad Destin woman seated last night and from which Miss Destin seemed so weirdly to have disappeared. She lifted the seat cushion, and there (it's almost like a splash of blood, Lida thought) lay the cerise handbag which Laura Destin had carried. "*Oh!*" Lida said, thoroughly shocked.

"You are hurt?"

"It's her handbag."

Lida picked up the bag and replaced the chair cushion. "Whose?" Godfrey asked.

"Laura Destin's."

"Impossible! Why do you say it is?"

"The color. You couldn't mistake it. Oh, Mr. Lance, don't you see what it means? She never left here."

"I tell you it is settled that she *did* leave here. It is all agreed."

"Never. Not without her bag. No woman would."

We are going to have trouble with this little chit, Godfrey thought. He repressed an immediate desire to either give her a sound spanking or choke her. He forced such delightful follies firmly to one side and said with the calmest sort of moderation: "You must remember that she is mad. What is it Hugo calls it? A persecution complex."

"I don't care what sort of a complex. I still don't believe she would have gone away without her bag." Godfrey loomed quite close to Lida.

"Miss Belder, you are beginning to interest me," he said.

"I think she must have been frightened by something after she came in."

"Why?"

"Because she shoved the bag under the cushion to hide it."

This busy, nimble young brain! Godfrey would have liked nothing better than to crush it, in the manner with which it pleased him to crush such summer insects as offended his comfort. How infinitely more Gestapo she was becoming than Hugo had been.

And dangerous. For Hugo had had his own skin to look out for, in a community sense, as had the rest of them.

He said judicially: "Yes, with a normal person such would be a logical deduction. But Laura Destin is not normal." (How like Hugo, he hoped, he was beginning to sound!) "Hugo has told us that the vagaries indulged in by psychopathic cases are legion, and that the persecution complex is especially unpredictable."

"But it's Miss Destin who's persecuting Aunt Christine. You're trying to make it appear the other way around."

"Only," Godfrey all but shouted in complete exasperation, "after Christine had persecuted her first! We can be sure that some shadow, some sound coming in from the forest, must have startled Miss Destin into protecting her bag by concealing it. And then, overwhelmed by this self-suggested fear, she fled in panic from the house. Forever gone!"

"Well, I don't see why you say she must have fled into the forest if that's where the sound came from that frightened her. Mr. Lance, you just don't make sense."

Godfrey gritted his teeth. He suppressed one of his favorite oaths. He said as calmly as possible: "I suggest that you leave the bag in the desk drawer and forget about it. If Miss Destin should come back—although I feel positive that she will not—we will give it to her."

"Well-all right."

Lida put the bag in a desk drawer as Alan started drearily coming down the turret stairs. He was haggard from lack of sleep, and his skin looked chalky above the flaming dressing gown which he wore. He walked lethargically toward the door to Christine's suite. Even he knew that what little brain he possessed was completely numb, and he didn't care.

"Good morning," Lida said brightly.

Alan gave her a sour smile. He said: "I doubt it."

"Why do you not go to bed and get some sleep?" Godfrey asked.

"My head is splitting."

Godfrey smiled pursily and said: "Nothing that a happy picnic will not cure."

"Oh God!"

Alan went into Christine's rooms, and Godfrey said: "If he were not the viper which he is, I could almost feel sorry for him. Come, I will make you your coffee."

"I'll be right with you as soon as I empty these ash trays."

"Very well."

Godfrey left the room, and Lida swiftly dumped the ash trays into a jardiniere beside the desk. Then she took the cerise handbag from the drawer and opened it.

On top of its clutter of contents lay the gold casing of a lipstick. A part of the cosmetic stuck out. It was roughly edged. Lida looked at the floor below the armchair, where the bag had been. She saw, pressed into the rose-toned rug where a foot had crushed it, the broken-off end of the lipstick.

A probable scene unfolded. Lida felt she could almost vision it as it might have occurred: the woman sitting in the chair where she had left her, already nervous and on edge, then a nervous attempt to repair her make-up: the cerise bag opened and the lipstick taken out, the mirror held and the cosmetic in the act of being applied to her lips when—Well?

It could have been a number of things, but each, to have snapped the stick off in that fashion, must have been violently startling in nature.

Startled?

Could it not have been struck from her hand?

What lay in back of that sudden desire for concealing the bag, which must have been an almost reflex response to the fright?

Lida poked further within the bag. She found a folder outlining the allures of Texas as a winter resort. In a separate compartment were some bills. There were three five-hundred-dollar bills. A shiver ran through Lida: no, never in the world would the woman have voluntarily left that bag. There were a car registration and a driver's license. The name on them was Belle Crystal, the address an upper-west-side one in New York. An alias, of course. But even so...

Faintly Lida heard the front-door chime ring. She closed the bag and decided not to put it back in the desk. She put it instead where she had found it, under the cushion of the chair where the woman had sat.

She went out and along the hallway to the entrance hall. She opened the front door.

A state trooper faced her.

CHAPTER XV

The trooper looked wonderfully secure to Lida: a sane and solid rock in this foggy sea of vague and disturbing conjectures.

"Sergeant Emmett Asher," he said to her factually. "I would like to speak with Miss Cordelia Banning."

"Miss Banning has gone shopping."

"Then I will see Mrs. Admont, please."

"Come in, Sergeant Asher."

"Thank you."

He followed her back into the morning room, where Lida said: "I will let her know," and went into Christine's suite. He casually looked the room over as he removed his gauntlets and shoved them under his belt.

Godfrey's portrait of Christine staggered Asher into a closer look, but it was a near-by Fragonard that soundly scandalized him. Truly the rich had small shame. His wife would never have permitted such a subject (the painting depicted a healthy faun in full chase after three all-but-veiled nymphs who weren't hurrying any faster than they had to) inside the Asher home at the Notch. In spite of all that he had heard about her, he could hardly believe that the canvas had been Mrs. Admont's choice.

He shrugged in disgusted disapproval as Christine came in with Alan and Lida.

"Sergeant Asher?" Christine said cordially. "How do you do? This is my husband, Alan Admont. Miss Belder, I believe, you have met."

"Good morning, Mr. Admont," Asher said, not liking him at all. That was the jerk, he decided, who had picked out the Fragonard.

Alan didn't help matters any by saying: "Is it?" and then going over to the lounge and sprawling out on it full length.

"The dear man is walking in his sleep," Christine said. "Up all night. Well, let us sit down."

"Mr. Lance has promised me some coffee," Lida said. "Perhaps Sergeant Asher will have some. Will you?"

"Thank you," Asher said, "no."

"Godfrey roasts the fresh beans himself. So sensible. Then he grinds them for drip." Christine turned to Lida. "Thank you, dear. The sergeant won't."

Lida left them, and Asher said: "I am here about one of your guests, Mrs. Admont. Miss Cordelia Banning."

"So Lida told me. Well, do sit down." Christine gauged his frame. She indicated one of the more stolid of the chairs. "Sit there." She waited until Sergeant Asher had filled it and then said: "Now what about Miss Banning?"

"Are you familiar with Jerbutt's jewelry shop in Vanderkill, Mrs. Admont?"

Christine's wickedly smart eyebrows rose a quarter of an inch. "I am not."

"It is like this. On yesterday afternoon Mr. Jerbutt was showing a customer in the rear of his shop some objects suitable for bridge prizes. Just then a woman came in and stood at the counter that has his engagement rings. This counter is in the front of the store, and it was, as you may remember, a foggy and dark afternoon."

"Wasn't it?" Christine agreed brightly. "Such a dull season of the year, fall. Especially in the mountains. So hard to know how to dress."

"This woman," Asher went on relentlessly, "looked a little familiar to Mr. Jerbutt, but by the time he had persuaded his customer to choose the bronze ash tray the woman up front had gone."

"Are you inferring that Mr. Jerbutt thought the woman to have been Miss Banning?"

"Not right then. That is, he wasn't certain of it. In fact, he still isn't quite certain of it."

Alan groaned.

"Is your husband ill?" Asher asked punctiliously.

"I am never ill," Alan said coldly. "I have never been sick in my life. I just want a drink."

"Go to sleep, dear," Christine said. "This is really most involved, Sergeant Asher."

"I know it is. Anyhow, Mr. Jerbutt remembered he had forgotten to put away a tray of engagement rings. He had been showing them to a man when the bridge-prize customer came in. He looked and saw that one of the rings was gone. It was a half-carat number set in platinum. The best ring he had. He went out onto the street just in case the woman might still be in sight, but she wasn't."

"This is sounding more and more like abracadabra. Also I am beginning to feel a trifle annoyed, Sergeant."

"Don't be. I'm handling it this way because people have a liking for you around here. They respect your position. They look on you in Dour Notch as a landmark."

Christine suppressed a delighted shriek.

"Sergeant, I've been called a thousand things, but never that. Seriously, I appreciate what you mean, and I appreciate your approach, only for heaven's sake do approach it."

"Well, Mr. Jerbutt didn't see the woman, but he did see your station wagon parked next door, in front of the Au Gourmet Meat Market. It reminded him of Miss Banning, and that reminded him that the woman who had come into his shop and gone out could have looked like Miss Banning."

"How on earth could be know what Miss Banning looks like? I'm sure we've never dealt there."

"Miss Banning, in Vanderkill, is quite well known. To be frank, Mrs. Admont, a good many little articles have been missed as she shops around. The stores don't mind it, as they don't want to lose the Belder Tor patronage. They just make it up on the bill. But with Mr. Jerbutt, you see, there was no patronage. And it wasn't only the diamond ring. Another piece of diamond jewelry had been lifted the week before."

"I find this utterly unbelievable, don't you? Miss Banning comes from one of the best-known families in New York. In fact, one of her extremely early forebears was a mayor."

"That never makes any difference. Sometimes they're the worst."

"But the thing is absurd. You say yourself that the light in the store was dim and that Mr. Jerbutt considered the woman to be only faintly familiar in appearance."

"It was somewhat more definite than that. He went into the meat market and introduced himself to Miss Banning. He asked her point blank whether or not she had just been in his shop. She said no."

"Well, then?"

"She said she never considered jewelry other than Tiffany's. Which made Mr. Jerbutt madder."

"Yes, I can see where it would. But didn't that end it?"

"It would have if Miss Banning had been wearing her gloves."

"Gloves?"

"Yes, she was carrying them. Mr. Jerbutt was sore enough to look on the glass top of the showcase for fingerprints, and he found a set of beauties. He called us in and had us photograph them."

"The glass tops in Mr. Jerbutt's store must be littered with fingerprints."

"Possibly, but the ones beside the tray of engagement rings were exceptionally distinct."

"They could have been those of the man who had been examining the rings."

"It's doubtful, because they were small and delicate. And the point is this. If they *are* Miss Banning's, Jerbutt is going to swear out a warrant. I told him I'd come here and talk it over with her. You can see what I mean?"

"No, Sergeant, I can't."

"It's this. If Miss Banning would let us have her prints willingly of her own accord, we would know that she was in the clear. If she won't, Mr. Jerbutt intends to swear out the warrant and get her fingerprints when she is booked."

"Booked. What a beastly word." Christine thought for a moment and then smiled brightly. "Cordelia is such a shrinking soul. A thing like this would upset her dismally and she wouldn't be a bit of use to anybody for weeks. May I suggest something?"

"I wish you would, Mrs. Admont."

"Come with me to Miss Banning's room. Surely the drinking glass, any number of small objects must have her fingerprints on them. Select any one you like and take it with you. In that way she need know nothing about it, and you can disprove this stupid accusation to Mr. Jerbutt's satisfaction."

"Yes, I could do that."

"You will also tell him for me that if there is any further mention of this I will see that Miss Banning brings suit for defamation of character." Christine stood up. She headed for the turret stairs. She said to Asher: "Come!"

CHAPTER XVI

Alan opened his eyes after Christine and Sergeant Asher had gone. His brain was no longer numb. He was in a thoroughly villainous mood. The night had been an interminable nightmare throughout which every nerve had been on edge against that worst possible of all menaces: the unknown. A dozen times or more some joint within the tired old house had creaked, and Alan had braced himself to face the Dove and, if reason failed to prevail, to kill him.

But the Dove had not materialized.

How simple, how *right* the scheme had seemed when he had discussed it yesterday morning with Joe! Alan groaned and stood up. Then in a flash it occurred to him that this moment was the first one which had offered itself for a search of Christine's rooms. For the quick-freezer key. He ran to the turret stairs and looked up them. Surely he had several minutes before she and Asher would come down.

He ran into her rooms and began a feverish and completely futile search. He located the house gown she had been wearing, but the key was no longer in its pocket. His irritation mounted heavily as he wondered where the old spider had put it.

In one dresser drawer there was a bunch of keys on a ring. Maybe one of them would fit. He ran back into the morning room and over to the freezer door. He tried several of the keys without results. He heard Christine's voice floating down the turret stairs. He jammed the ring of keys into the pocket of his dressing gown and threw himself again flat onto the lounge.

Sergeant Asher was carrying a glass tumbler wrapped in a handkerchief. He assured Christine that he could find the front door. He said good-by.

Christine looked after him regretfully.

"Such a sturdy man!"

Alan looked at her spitefully.

"So you threw Cordelia to the wolves," he said.

"*No*, dear. I simply took him into Lida's room instead of Cordelia's. I let him pick out a glass which Lida had handled, and that will end the matter."

"Christine, I am speechless."

"I must speak to Cordelia about checking the bills more closely."

"You'd better also tell her to brush up on her technique."

"Do go up and finish dressing, Alan. We'll leave for the picnic as soon as Hugo and Cordelia get back." Alan groaned. He stood up.

"Darling—must we?"

"Put on something warm, dear."

"Christine."

"Yes?"

"I've thought about this a lot during the night," Alan said earnestly, almost desperately. "Are we happy here at Belder Tor? Are *you* happy?"

"Very happy, Alan. Why?"

"You're not. This is no life for you. It's no life for either of us, Christine. Always you've done things on the spur of the moment, and so have I. Let's do it now."

"But do what?"

Alan blurted it out tensely: "Flee to Mexico."

"Flee?"

"Yes, from this life of stagnation. Think of it—sunshine, music, gaiety—just the two of us together in some quiet little nook on the Pacific Ocean where nobody could bother us or find us."

"You'd be sick of it in a week. And I'd be sick of it in about one hour. Mexico City, of course—"

Alan pounced gratefully.

"All right, even Mexico City."

"Why, yes. Why not?"

"Thank God! We'll go today—we'll go right now!"

"Ridiculous!" Christine looked at him in speculative amazement. "The Vanbuskirks are coming, and there's Lida's wedding. We will run down for Christmas, and if we like it we can take a place for the balance of the winter. Now go up and put your things on, dear."

Alan plunged swiveling into a deflation of black despair.

"And now," he cried, "do the gods with their laughter fill the skies!"

Yes, he thought, not bad. He embellished the exit with a Pagliacci laugh and ran tragically up the turret stairs.

Christine looked after him fondly. Such a comfort to have him around. Exhilarating. Far simpler than ocean plunges or any daily dosage of vitamin D.

CHAPTER XVII

Lida finished a wholesome arrangement of coffee, toast, and eggs. It was remarkable how the meal burnished and brightened up her dark thoughts. Reason told her that in an ordinary household the popping in and out of Laura Destin would have been a seventh-wonder event. But not at Belder Tor. Even the bag. No. Lida still held reservations about the bag.

Godfrey made the flat statement that he would at once start blocking her in. He took her into the studio, where he encased his very large body in (necessarily) a very large artist's smock.

The studio had formerly been Belder Tor's ballroom and was quite large. Its windows faced the north, which was about all that could be said for them as an aid to painting, especially with the dismal grayness of the day. An easel and a palette stand were near them and, at some distance, a platform on which stood a Moorish chair.

"How can you see in here?" Lida asked.

"I don't have to. I feel."

Godfrey went to a handsome reproducing machine and switched it on. He fiddled with the volume control and a whisper of gloom sifted dismally through the room. Lida decided it was Bach at his melancholy best.

"I cannot paint," Godfrey said to her, "without mood. Sit up on that chair, please."

"In any special pose?"

"It does not matter. I do not look at you."

He went to the easel. He selected a brush. His eyes contemplated broodingly the window's dreary shroud.

"Miss Belder," he said, "what is your opinion of murder?"

Lida, in reflex, took a stronger grip on the arms of the Moorish chair.

"I am," she quoted decisively, "against it."

"Please! If your psychoses are to be exposed, we must not quibble. I will be more specific. There are so many kinds of murder. For passion, for greed, for fear." He padded the brush in cerulean blue. He said quietly: "And for security."

"Security?"

"Yes. Can you understand that? Take the normal course of one's life. If you have a disease, you swallow medicine and you kill the germs which are preventing a rightfully contented existence. Now admit that everything is relative. A person attacks you for his own selfish interests in a fashion which would destroy your wellbeing in a manner similar to a disease. So you kill him as, with medicine, you would kill a germ. For your security. What is the difference?"

"That is sophistry. With a person you have recourse to law, and with a disease, a doctor."

No, Godfrey thought darkly, she could never be a kindred soul. Never (he saw this plainly now) could she be drawn into the group. Well, he would have to talk the problem over with the others. So far he had had no chance. But either during or after the picnic he would do so. Then they could all decide what would be best. For them.

"I was right," he said coldly. "You are definitely a cerulean blue."

He said nothing further. He did not look at her. His brush made strokes on the canvas, and Bach gloomed endlessly on. An auto horn sounded faint in the outer chill.

Godfrey put down his brushes.

"There are Cordelia and Hugo," he said. "Tomorrow morning will finish you. I can waste no more time. You may go up now, Miss Belder, and put your things on for this putrid picnic which will shortly commence. This canvas will be one of my best, and I shall sell it to Christine for a good big sum."

Lida went upstairs to her room, and the first thing which struck her was the fact that the diamond clip was no longer on the dresser. She knew perfectly well she had left it there and for a moment wondered whether a dash of Indian had caused Cordelia to take it back. Scarcely, since Cordelia had gone shopping before Lida had put it on the bureau top.

She put on a sweater, finished a few odd tidyings of her room, and then went out into the hallway and knocked on Cordelia's door.

Cordelia's aunt-like face lighted up with pleasure when Lida came in.

"Oh, I do feel so much better," Cordelia said. "Such a stuffy night. The air and the drive this morning did me a world of good. And there *is* something so exhilarating about shopping, don't you think? Even if it's just for little things."

"I feel it mostly about hats."

"Yes, I know. But sometimes even a selection between cutlets can have its excitement. Do sit down."

Lida sat down.

She said: "I've been wanting to talk with you about the diamond clip you gave me, Miss Banning. I know it must have been a keepsake or an heirloom, and I wanted to give it back to you."

"Nonsense. The pleasure I get from giving little things to my friends is far beyond their memories to me. I insist that you keep it."

"This is awfully embarrassing, but I put the clip on my dresser this morning so that I would remember to return it to you, and now it's gone."

"Gone, dear?"

"Yes, and I remember the exact spot where I put it."

"How very odd." A queer look came over Cordelia's kind face and she said suddenly: "When are you marrying Barry, Lida?"

"On Friday, unless we can arrange everything sooner."

"You will not think me strange if I say something?" Then Cordelia added with a dreadful sort of earnestness: "You will not repeat it, dear?"

"Of course I won't."

"I am going to suggest that the instant Barry reaches here this afternoon you get in his car and go. Think up whatever excuse you can, or simply make it an elopement, but go. Go, dear, and get married *today*!"

"Oh, I *never* could do that to Aunt Christine, Miss Banning."

Cordelia seemed suddenly flaccid and, in spite of her plumpness, thin.

"No," she said, "it is difficult for anyone to do anything for—"

She did not complete the sentence because the door opened abruptly and Christine came in. Christine was, incidentally, expertly and superbly dressed for a picnic. In the very best fall tones.

"Lida," Christine said, "I've been looking all over for you. I heard the sound of voices in here. Barry telephoned. They'll be here early this afternoon and will stay overnight. Cordelia darling, we can open up the rooms next to Hugo's, don't you think? Do you mind, dear, if you were to attend to it right after we get back from the picnic?"

"I will see that the rooms are prepared, Christine."

CHAPTER XVIII

The picnic began.

It was an involved affair, as everything which Christine arranged for was involved, and necessitated the use of many baskets. The procession started from the terrace, with its destination a particularly uneventful flat rock at the lake shore, with an outdoor fireplace that was to do the trick on the chickens and corn.

Belder Tor was alone.

The Catskill Mountains were not at their best. Thunderheads loomed over Roundtop, and the closer sky was a lowering gray. Blankets were spread on the flat rock and a fire shortly leaped into flame on the outdoor hearth.

Christine's accurate eye surveyed the scene. Alan was busily absorbed in mixing cocktails. Godfrey was arranging chickens on the grill. Cordelia was busy husking corn while Hugo, with sardonic precision, was collecting a stock of firewood.

"I wonder," Christine said to Lida, "whether you would mind doing a little thing for me, dear?"

"Of course not, Aunt Christine."

"The air is chillier than I had thought. Would you go back to the house and bring me my beaver jacket?" Christine opened her bag and took a tagged key from it. "Here, dear. It is in the freezer locker. The door I locked last night."

Belder Tor, when Lida neared it, seemed curiously dead. She went by way of the terrace and caught, just as she opened a french door of the morning room, the ringing of the telephone bell. She ran over to the spinet desk, and Barry's voice came back at her as she lifted the handset and said: "Hello?"

He was, he told her, at Kingston. Complete with parents. He had slaughtered the Chelsea aunts as the simplest means of getting rid of them, so they had had an earlier start than had been expected.

Right now they were at lunch. They would continue on to Belder Tor at its conclusion.

"And we," Lida told him, "are having a picnic down by the lake. I just ran back to get Aunt Christine's beaver jacket."

He asked her whether the night had been made hideous by screams, and she said no: nothing but a mysterious cerise-colored bag which she would tell him about when he got there. They said good-by.

Lida unlocked and opened the freezer door.

A wave of cold shoved against her. The light which Hugo had turned on was still lighted. She stepped inside and looked for beaver.

She saw the woman's face.

Even as horror wrenched her, the smear of lipstick across the woman's lips pinged her consciousness. The cosmetic had streaked down from the right corner of the mouth, giving the dead mask the grotesqueness of a tragic grimace. Sharply the realization came to Lida that her conjectures, on finding the cerise bag, had been correct: the woman, as she had been applying the lipstick, *had* been struck a blow across the mouth, for the flesh above the lip was slightly lacerated as if it had been raked by a bit of metal.

Lida thought she had screamed, but she had not. The sound had been constricted within her throat. She left the locker and shut its door. She left the key in its lock.

Dizziness suddenly overcame her as she stumbled toward the desk to telephone the police. She sank onto the desk chair and tried to ward off fainting by applying the usual home remedy of lowering her head down between her knees.

Lida was in this ungainly position when the door to Christine's suite started to open. She caught sight of the moving door and sat up. No one but herself was in the house. The door couldn't be opening. But it was.

She observed the door stupidly and saw an elderly, gentlemanly looking man, quietly dressed in dove-toned grays and wearing a fedora hat, step in. He carried a businesslike-looking brief case in one of his silk-gloved hands.

The man started almost imperceptibly as he saw Lida and stood still. He took off his hat.

He said in a gentle, cultured voice: "I hope I haven't alarmed you. I was certain that everyone would be out of the house because of the picnic for at least another hour." He took a step nearer to her. "Are you well? Your face is very pale."

Lida, through her recurring waves of nausea, tried to place him. There was something very reassuring about him, in the way that Sergeant Asher had been reassuring. Her sick, shocked mind seized this as a life belt.

She said impulsively: "I know. It's about Miss Banning. Are you connected with Sergeant Asher? I was about to telephone the police."

The man's gentle voice hardened and he said swiftly: "Do not. Yes, I am a detective. Tell me what the trouble is."

Lida's feeling of relief was almost pitiful.

She said, "There is a dead woman in that freezer." The Dove, again gentle, walked calmly to a french door, opened it, took a leisurely look toward the picnic grounds, then closed the door again. He drew a chair over close to Lida and sat down.

"Now tell me. Just tell me all about it."

Lida, on this closer view of him, thought his skin peculiarly white: of that unattractive pallor found in people whose job or fancy prevents them from the sun.

"Aunt Christine was cold and asked me to fetch her a fur," she said. "She gave me the key to the locker."

"Have you the key with you now?"

"It's in the door."

"I see." The Dove added soothingly: "Are you quite certain that you did not call the police?"

"Yes. I was just going to when I felt faint. It was the way she looked that sickened me. There's a cut on her lip as if someone had struck her across her mouth. The lipstick's all smeared down."

"Who is she?"

"She's a woman who has been threatening Aunt Christine for years. Her name is Laura Destin. She came last night and wanted to see Aunt Christine, but she wasn't here when we came back into the room." Sickness again started to engulf Lida and she added miserably: "And that's all."

"All?"

"Well, no one admits to seeing her again after I left her here, and they all insisted she had gone away because she was insane. But she couldn't have, because she left her handbag and she's in there dead."

"She—she left her handbag?"

"I found it this morning when I was helping Mr. Lance to straighten up the room. It has her alias in it on her driver's license and car registration cards. Belle Crystal."

The Dove for a moment closed his gentle eyes. He felt bitterly disturbed and put out. For the first time in his exemplary career he found himself confused. That was the trouble, of course, with moving out of one's class, one's familiar little circle.

He should have refused Joe right at the start, should have told Joe he wouldn't even consider any proposition involving these hybrids. During his jobs on good dependable gangsters he had always known precisely where he stood. The unpredictable had been an absent factor.

Certainly there had been no picnics where the principal in the case had felt cold and wanted a fur coat. There had been no clavichords which the principal alone had been supposed to play but which had suddenly produced a second performer. Nor any Prunelle liqueur, reserved for the principal, and then, after the remainder of the drink had been well spiked with poison, dumped unceremoniously onto the floor by a klepto-dipsomaniac.

Nor, even before Belle, had any of Joe's women ever poked her nose into the orderly procedure of the day.

"Where," the Dove sighed, "is the bag now, please?"

"It's under the cushion of that chair, where she had hidden it." Lida glanced toward the freezer door and shuddered. "I knew she never would have gone away without it."

The Dove lifted the chair cushion and picked up the cerise handbag.

"Aren't you going to telephone?" Lida asked him.

"Why?"

"Don't you always telephone headquarters and have the homicide squad sent out?"

The Dove started to open Belle's handbag.

"There will be plenty of time."

"Oh!" Lida wailed, the thought just striking her.

It was a good loud wail, and the Dove, startled, shut the hand-bag and faced her.

"You have thought of something?" he said.

"Barry's driving his mother and father here. They ought to be here in under an hour. Oh, can't we stop them?"

"Why?"

"Why! It's such a horrible—I mean, how would *you* feel? They've never even met!"

The Dove did not even attempt to sort this out. He said: "In under an hour." He put his brief case, hat, and Belle's bag down on the desk.

"Yes. Didn't you hear the telephone?"

"Not with the doors closed."

Lida suddenly began to be not quite satisfied.

"What were you doing in Aunt Christine's rooms, anyhow?"

The Dove gently flexed his fingers.

"Arranging—that is, examining some things."

"But Miss Banning's room is upstairs."

"You will understand that in my profession I cannot talk quite freely?"

"Of course," Lida agreed, still not liking it.

"Are you feeling a little stronger now?"

The Dove's manner was most soothing and greatly restored Lida's initial feeling of confidence and security.

"Oh, I'm all right with you here. It was just the first shock that made me feel faint."

The outer day had been slowly darkening as the thunderheads moved nearer from Roundtop. The room, correspondingly, had slowly darkened too.

The Dove thought: She will have to be silenced. Without dispute that fact was the beginning and the period to his problem. He gave himself somewhere in the neighborhood of ten or fifteen more minutes before the others would wonder why she had not returned to the picnic. Before then she would have to disappear.

How difficult it was. Her vanishment from life was an entirely different matter than that of a woman like Belle. Belle was just a friend of Joe's who wouldn't show up again, as other of his friends had failed to do. Without any later or annoying remarks.

But this girl had a Barry who was no Joe. Barry would yell his head off and rip things through the middle until his rage and grief would have got at the vitals of it. Possibly the entire Vanbuskirk clan would bring their powerful batteries into play.

And Barry's road would lead via the weak-sister Alan to Joe, and then via Joe to the Dove. His confusion deepened. He could not let her go and himself walk out, and thus happily wash his pale white hands of the whole messed-up affair. Joe would get him for it if he did. Joe would get him through the offices of some other Dove.

Kill her now.

The method was of small consequence, when you came right down to it. Then conceal the body and at greater leisure devise a scheme for cutting this Gordian knot.

He stepped gently over to the quick-freezer door and opened it.

"I wonder whether you would mind?" he said.

"What?"

"Showing me just what you mean about the cut?"

Lida joined the Dove at the freezer door.

"Don't you see it?" she asked. "It's as if a sharp piece of metal had torn the upper lip."

The Dove sighed again, and his fingers closed with the force of steel around Lida's throat. From the position where they were standing he had a full view of the terrace windows and he heard, coming faintly from outdoors, Christine's voice calling: "Yoo-hoo—yoo-hoo! Oh, Lida dear—"

The Dove hurled Lida into the freezer and slammed its door. He locked it and shoved the tagged key into his coat pocket. He caught a glimpse of Christine out on the terrace. Swiftly he picked up his hat, brief case, and Belle's handbag from the desk.

He drifted up the turret stairs.

CHAPTER XIX

Christine was tired from hurrying, an act so rare that for a moment she caught her breath and sank into an armchair for a breathing spell. The room pressed dimly and quietly about her, and she wondered, as her eyes negligently rested on the terrace windows, what on earth Alan was running for. He all but burst into the hushed, storm-darkened room.

"Christine!" he shouted at the top of his lungs. Alan saw her in the armchair. "Oh—are you all right?"

"Certainly I am. I'm a little out of breath from hurrying, that's all."

In spite of his superb physique, Alan himself was a little winded. For a passing flash the fact annoyed him, but then, after all, when he considered what he'd been through! What he was *going* through.

He said: "Cordelia told me just now that when Lida took so long getting you whatever it was you wanted that you thought the Vanbuskirks might have got here ahead of time. She said you came up to welcome them."

"I did. Lida is a darling child, but I intend making every effort to see that this agreeable marriage takes place. And what spurred you into this three-alarm entrance, darling?"

Sarcastic old beast! thought Alan.

"I—I hurried to welcome them too," he said. "Where are they?"

"Evidently they haven't come."

"Where's Lida?"

"I don't know. Do you suppose she's all right? Go upstairs and see."

Never! Oh no, never would he leave this precious old lump alone down here in the storm-sultry gloom, an atmosphere so dismal that it could have been tailor-made for the Dove.

"I won't leave you down here alone," Alan said with truculence.

Christine was thoroughly aggravated and said sharply: "Will you stop this childish nonsense? Go up to her room and ask her whether she is all right.

Alan glanced with a shudder toward the freezer and silently asked heaven to give him strength. Where *was* the key to that wretched locker which Hugo, with all the éclat of a cretin, had selected as a good safe catacomb?

"You'll call, Christine, if you need me?"

"I will shriek. Alan, I think I will shriek anyhow if you don't stop worrying over the ridiculous possibility of Laura Destin's still being in the house."

Defeated, Alan squared his handsome shoulders and darted up the turret stairs.

Christine leaned back and closed her eyes, pressing her hands against them, and the dark sky burst as a nerve-shattering, earsplitting crash of thunder exploded the stillness. It shocked Christine thoroughly, and she stood up and went to a terrace window, where rain began to pelt down in a sudden mountain torrent.

How Charley, Christine thought, would have loved it. It always had brought out the Grieg in him, and he would insist that she vie with the thunder by pounding out, on the clavichord, the "Hall of the Mountain King." Christine left the window and turned on lamps as Cordelia, wet through, hurried breathlessly in from the terrace.

"It's a cloudburst," Cordelia said, hurrying right on to the turret stairs. "I'll have to change this dress." Godfrey and Hugo ran in. Both of them were panting. "Christine," Godfrey said with considerable pleasure, "the picnic is ruined, and thank God." He sneezed. He said: "I knew it!" and headed for the cellaret, where Hugo joined him.

"And where, Christine, are the happy lovebirds and the cortege of parents?" Hugo asked. "Not drowned, I hope."

"They haven't come yet, Hugo. Lida is upstairs in her room for some reason or other. I sent Alan up to see whether she was all right."

"What got into her?"

"I don't know. When she was gone for so long I felt sure that the Vanbuskirks must be here. Boston always *is* so previous."

Alan, about finished with panting, ran down the turret stairs.

"Christine, she isn't there," he said.

"How perfectly weird, Alan, she must be."

"Well, she isn't. I knocked a couple of times and then went right in." Alan eyed the slow drips of water fringing Godfrey and Hugo. "Have a pleasant swim?" he asked.

"I am getting right out of these clothes," Godfrey said sternly, "before I am attacked by pernicious pleurisy."

Hugo said: "Me too." Then he turned to Alan. "As for the tea-pot-tempest mystery of the disappearing Miss Belder, I leave it in your drier hands. I would suggest that she probably walked down the road to that view of the Notch in the roseate hope of glimpsing her young man's car."

"Hugo," Christine said, "that must be it."

Godfrey looked spitefully at Alan.

"If your chivalry feels like blooming a bit, you might go down the road and see. I advise the Australian crawl."

"Bring her back in a sponge," Hugo added as he and Godfrey dripped up the turret stairs.

"Why don't you, Alan," Christine said, "take her an umbrella?"

"I'll be damned if I will. She's still got her two feet." Alan flung himself into a chair. "I suppose the immediate program," he said petulantly, "is a slow starvation until Godfrey feels dry enough to cook lunch?"

"Oh, stop being so irritable, Alan. What's got into you lately?"

"I want to go to Mexico."

"Well, I told you that we would."

"I want to go *now*."

"Alan, we are staying right here until Christmas—and that is final."

They heard, above the lashing of the rain, the sound of some-one out on the terrace pounding on one of the french doors.

"What's the silly fool knocking for?" Alan said. "Why doesn't she come right in?"

"Oh, really, Alan!"

Christine opened the terrace door, and Stuyvesant Swain, very wet, very irritated, faced her.

"Stuyvesant darling—how nice!"

Stuyvesant came in and shook rain from his hat. "Christine, if it were not for my fond memories of Charley, I would wholeheartedly curse Belder Tor and everyone in it, including yourself. I rang that damned front doorbell for the duration of six shower baths, and nothing happened. So I came around here." He held out a wet hand. "How do you do?"

Christine took it and said, "It's dripping."

"And what did you expect? My car slewed off the road on that Vaseline-surfaced goat's path you call a driveway. It is now engagingly wedded to one pine tree and a Colorado blue spruce."

"Were you hurt?"

"Miraculously not. And don't try to cozen me with your crocodile sympathies, Christine." Stuyvesant bowed to Alan. "Mr. Admont, good afternoon."

Alan seized, and pumped, Stuyvesant's hand.

"Give me your coat and hat, Mr. Swain. I'll hang them in the kitchen near the range."

"Thank you." Stuyvesant handed them over. "You might first put them through the wringer."

"Will you help yourself to scotch? Right over there."

"I will."

Alan left, and Stuyvesant went over to the cellaret. Christine said, "This is most unexpected and quite delightful, Stuyvesant."

Stuyvesant mixed a drink and carried it over to the desk, where he sat down.

"Christine, I have worried about you consistently since leaving here last night."

"But why? Surely the annuity is a defense against everything?"

"Even so, I could not help it. During the night I dreamed of Charley. I saw him as clearly as I see you now. He said: 'Go to her, old man. She is in desperate danger.'"

"You must have been eating lobster."

"Well, I had. Then it was almost an omen this morning when a further question came up concerning the transfer of this property to the annuity fund. I had another paper for you to sign and put everything else aside and came. I could almost feel Charley standing at my elbow and urging me to."

"Dear Charley!"

"You never appreciated him."

"I did, and I loved him."

"Well, never mind." Stuyvesant spread a paper out on the desk and took out his pen. "Sign here."

Christine signed, and Stuyvesant put the paper back in his pocket.

"And where is your motley collection today, Christine?"

"They're in their rooms changing their clothes. We were having a picnic. Stuyvesant, I'm worried about her."

"About what her?"

"Lida."

"Surely your portrait-painting cook hasn't eaten her?"

"No, dear. It's simply that she seems to have disappeared."

"Christine, if such a trifle as a vanishing grandniece disturbs you, you must be slipping. Just what is this about Lida, anyhow?"

"I asked her to get me a fur, and it took so long—It's perfectly possible that she *did* walk down the road to look for the Vanbuskirks' car. Did you pass her along the road anywhere, Stuyvesant?"

"I passed no one. The girl, Christine, is a healthy outdoor creature. You will find that she is sheltering under a tree or in a cave from this typical Catskill cascade."

Again there came a pounding on one of the french doors from outside on the terrace.

Stuyvesant said flatly: "There she is now."

Christine opened the door, and Sergeant Asher, well wrapped in a glistening poncho, stepped in.

"I've been expecting this for years," Stuyvesant said with a groan. "The police!"

CHAPTER XX

"Sergeant Asher?" Christine said.

"Sorry to trouble you again, Mrs. Admont."

"For heaven's sakes, come in." Asher came in, and Christine shut the door. "This house is turning into an ark. That steaming gentleman with the highball is Stuyvesant Swain, my lawyer."

"How do you do, Mr. Swain?" Asher said punctiliously.

"Better join me in a highball, Sergeant."

"Not while on duty, thank you." Asher turned to Christine. "I would like to see Miss Belder and ask her a few questions about a diamond clip."

Cordelia started coming down the turret stairs. Stuyvesant groaned again. "I knew it," he muttered. "Charley, how right you were!"

Christine said to Asher, after giving Stuyvesant a look, "This is some more of Mr. Jerbutt's nonsense, I suppose? I can assure you that Miss Belder has never been in his shop. In fact she had never come to Belder Tor before yesterday."

Cordelia hesitated at the foot of the stairs, listening. Asher was not impressed. He said: "Miss Belder had on her dresser the diamond clip which had been lifted from Mr. Jerbutt's on the week previous to yesterday's theft of the ring."

"Nonsense. You have never been in my grandniece's room. You were in Miss Banning's."

"The room you took me into had silver toilet articles initialed L.B. and not C.B., and there was some correspondence on the bureau addressed to Miss Lida Belder."

"Christine," Stuyvesant said severely, "poor Charley must be spinning in his grave."

"Stuyvesant, you be still."

Asher went on doggedly: "Mrs. Admont, you practically established Miss Banning's guilt by deliberately steering me away from her fingerprints. The diamond clip ties Miss Belder in with the job. I took the clip to Jerbutt's for a definite identification."

Cordelia came into the room and went up to Asher. "Oh *dear*," she said, "I cannot let you implicate Miss Belder, Sergeant. I am the woman you want."

Stuyvesant announced: "Well, now, this is getting up to form, Christine."

"Oh, do keep quiet, Stuyvesant—and you too, Cordelia."

"No, Christine," Cordelia said, "I won't. I *was* in Mr. Jerbutt's shop, and I did pick up the diamond clip and the ring. I remember it perfectly now. Sergeant, I gave the clip last night to dear Lida as a little wedding gift." She held her dimpled hands out to Asher. "Put them on."

"Put what on, ma'am?"

"The handcuffs."

"What for? Mr. Jerbutt hasn't decided to swear out any warrant. He feels now, he says, that maybe Mrs. Admont can clear things up." Asher gave Stuyvesant a pointed look. "I don't need any glasses to see through *that*, of course."

"No," Stuyvesant agreed, "it has the old familiar sound."

Asher said to Christine: "I had to come out here and get a statement before closing my report."

"I am delighted that Mr. Jerbutt has come to his senses. Miss Banning is sometimes a little vague. Aren't you, dear?"

"I'm afraid I am," Cordelia said placidly.

"Sergeant Asher, I shall drive in and see Mr. Jerbutt. If necessary, I shall even open an account."

"I wouldn't use a car during this cloudburst, Mrs. Admont. The road down to the Notch is like grease."

"I shan't. I'll drive in in the morning."

"Well, then, everything is cleared up."

"Good-by, Sergeant Asher, and thank you."

"Good-by. Good-by, Miss Banning, and Mr. Swain." Asher left them, and Cordelia said to Stuyvesant how nice it was to see him again. Stuyvesant received this with a cold thank you and grew colder still as he saw Godfrey and Hugo come down the turret stairs.

"Good!" Godfrey cried on spotting Stuyvesant. "You have changed your mind. I knew that you could not resist."

"I have not changed my mind," Stuyvesant said between his teeth, "and I will not, Mr. Lance, be embalmed for posterity in puce."

"Christine," Godfrey implored, "persuade him."

"Don't bother me for a minute, Godfrey."

Christine frowned. It was queer, she thought, that even Sergeant Asher hadn't seen Lida on his way to Belder Tor. She noted absently that Alan had come back from the kitchen and was of two minds about sending him out into the downpour to search. Her eyes were speculative on the freezer door. She walked over and put her hand tentatively on the knob. She tried it and found it locked.

"Christine!" Hugo said sharply. "What are you doing?" Not only he but also Godfrey and Cordelia and Alan were stricken into immobility with the sickening feeling that fate was at last about to catch up with them.

"Well, really, Hugo! The possibility struck me that the door might have closed on her."

Stuyvesant felt a genuine alarm.

"On Lida, Christine?"

"Yes. But it's locked, and you can't lock it from the inside."

Hugo's voice in the tense stillness was strained: "Why would Miss Belder go there?"

"I asked her to get me my beaver jacket."

"Oh dear!" Cordelia moaned.

"I gave her the key to the freezer."

Cordelia wailed more earnestly still: "Oh, the poor child!" and collapsed onto the lounge in a faint.

Alan took it hardest of all. This, then, was the end. Like lightning the gall of his tragic future tore through his tottering brain: that cool, efficient young snip had undoubtedly opened the freezer door and found the body. No wonder they couldn't find Lida. She was of a certainty hotfooting it for the police, and only moments remained before all would be exposed. He was dully aware of Hugo's feeble efforts at staving catastrophe off.

"But Miss Belder couldn't be in the freezer, Christine," Hugo was saying.

"Not with the door locked," Godfrey boomed. "Christine, you said so yourself."

"Christine," Stuyvesant said stuffily, "if you don't mind my mentioning it, Miss Banning seems to have fainted."

"Well, I don't see why she should. Get the bottle of smelling salts, Alan."

"Where is it?"

"In the medicine chest in my bathroom."

Hugo went over to the lounge and looked professionally at Cordelia. "Bring a glass of water too, Alan."

"Your servant, sirrah—and madam." Alan floated through his shattered dreams toward the door to Christine's suite. He knew that no longer was anything of any use, and this irretrievable collapse of his golden future hurled him into the ultimate depths and—oh, bitterest pill of all!—it had hinged on a whim: Christine had wanted a fur coat. He hated her at that moment as he had never hated anyone on earth. With his hammiest irony he repeated his triumphal cry of the morning before: "The world is mine!" flung open Christine's door, and left the room.

Stuyvesant looked after Alan in bewilderment.

"Who does he think he is?" he asked Christine. "Booth?"

"Usually."

"Is Cordelia all right, Hugo?" Godfrey asked. "Certainly. It's nothing. She is coming around by herself."

"Water," Cordelia murmured weakly. "Water—"

Then she added, less weakly, "Or something—"

"Alan is getting you some," Hugo said.

There was a moment's hush, then breaking it they heard the sound of Alan's voice coming from Christine's suite in a shriek of outraged pain. There was a wailing quality about it which swelled to a sobbing scream then tapered off to the whimper of a child, and the room was still again.

CHAPTER XXI

They stood like dummies, completely spellbound by Alan's scream, their eyes fastened on the opened door to Christine's suite. It began to filter through to them that, simultaneously with the scream, the lights had sunk down, wavered, and were now at a low dim. Godfrey was the first to become fully conscious of this.

"What is happening to the lights?" he asked. Stuyvesant suggested caustically that a more pertinent question might be what was happening to Mr. Admont.

"There's a short circuit," Hugo said. "Some extra load. Come with me, Godfrey."

Godfrey followed Hugo into Christine's suite.

"They go down like this during an electrocution," Cordelia announced placidly. "While the juice is on."

"Oh, really, Cordelia!" Christine snapped, and followed Godfrey and Hugo.

"Didn't somebody scream, Mr. Swain?" Cordelia asked.

"Yes, Mr. Admont screamed. A natural pitch, I might presume, for his voice. He had gone into Christine's bathroom to get you some smelling salts and a glass of water." The lights jumped up suddenly to full.

"*Just*," Cordelia said, sitting up, "like an electrocution."

"The wiring is dangerous in most of these old houses."

"Yes, I remember that dear Margaret Lepstoad almost died from a shock she got from her curling iron. She lived in Mystic, Connecticut."

Christine rejoined them. She was obviously badly shaken. She went directly to the cellaret and picked up a bottle of scotch. Her hand was trembling so that she couldn't pour it.

"Pour this for me, please, Stuyvesant."

Stuyvesant poured the scotch.

"What did he yell for, Christine?"

"Alan has been killed."

Cordelia was sincerely horrified.

"Oh no!"

"Was it a short circuit?" Stuyvesant asked.

"Yes. His hand was glued to the bathroom tap. Hugo took bath towels and pulled him away." Christine downed the scotch. "There was some break in the heater cord, and a live wire was touching the water pipe."

"At the present moment," Stuyvesant said pompously, "the exact statistics do not occur to me, but the death rate from accidents in households each year is terrific." A shocking thought suddenly occurred to him. "Christine, it was your bathroom. It might have happened to you."

"Do you suppose I haven't thought of that?"

Cordelia stood up and went over to her.

"Christine dear, I'm so sorry."

"About Alan?"

"For your loss."

Stuyvesant became stuffily formal.

"My sympathies too, Christine." Then he added, unable to control it: "Although I don't mind saying I think you're damn well out of it."

"Mr. *Swain*!" Cordelia was gently reproachful. "I shall go and help Godfrey and Hugo. There must be pennies on his eyes."

Cordelia went into Christine's suite, and Stuyvesant said sternly: "The authorities should be notified at once, and the body must not be moved until they get here."

"Oh, don't be so technical, Stuyvesant!"

"Technical! Christine, fate and fate alone brought me back here this afternoon. I shall protect you in spite of yourself. Charley would wish me to."

He followed Cordelia into Christine's suite. Christine put down her empty whisky glass and, going to a terrace window, looked out at the pelting rain.

The Dove came down the turret stairs and into the room. He had put Belle's handbag into his brief case, and he spotted the motionless Christine just as Christine spotted him.

Confusion piled on confusion for the Dove. He felt caught like a leaf in a strong and variable wind. This sudden and face-to-face meeting with his principal thoroughly annoyed him.

Christine herself felt somewhat strange as she took in more accurately this wisp, this gray-haired wraith who was standing still now and facing her. After all, even for Back Bay—"Surely," she said, gathering about her some shreds of her social wits, "then you did get here. But where are Mrs. Vanbuskirk and Barry, and Lida?"

The Dove moved gently toward her, and there was a subtle menace in his steps which, subconsciously, Christine felt. He gave her a long look and then glanced reflectively over his shoulder toward the freezer door. He thought, with exasperated finality: I'll choke her now and add her to the collection.

Christine felt herself being swept further out to sea by the man's silence and gentle advance. She fought against the unusual sense of alarm and said to this hopelessly un-Bostonian incompetent: "It—it *is* Mr. Vanbuskirk, are you not?" She held out a welcoming hand and added: "How do you do?"

The Dove ignored it. He said: "Where are the others?" Christine started to ice.

"They are in my rooms. There has been an accident. My husband has just been killed."

The Dove stopped dead in his gentle, menacing tracks. His thin shoulders registered one resigned shrug and he gave what easily could have been taken for a low, sepulchral laugh.

"You find it amusing?" Christine said coldly.

The Dove smiled sadly.

He said: "I am thinking of the futility of the best-laid plans—of rats and men."

He went swiftly over to the spinet desk. He took hold of the telephone and yanked its cord free from the baseboard. Christine observed him with swiftly mounting outrage.

"Will you be good enough to tell me just what you think you are doing?" she managed to ask.

"My services here," the Dove said gently, "are of no further use."

Christine was standing before the terrace door, blocking it, as the Dove drifted politely toward her.

"I insist," she said, "upon an explanation for this extraordinary conduct!"

The Dove had reached her by now. He took her by the elbows and, with curious strength, moved her aside from the door. Outrage flamed into fire. Christine's sheltered if hectic existence had never included any experience even remotely connected with being man-handled. Dear Charles, it is true, had once thrown a book, but the book had missed her, and these bony fingers now so impertinently gripping her drove her into fury.

"Mr. Vanbuskirk," she said bitingly, "I have had enough. There is a limit. Even during these mad and equivocal days a hostess can be stretched too far."

The Dove, too, had had enough.

"I am not," he said between clenched teeth, "Mr. Vanbuskirk."

"Then—who?"

"I am a man who inadvertently has done you, madam, an inestimable service."

The Dove sifted out onto the terrace, quietly closing the rain-streaked french door.

CHAPTER XXII

Stuyvesant came in and, after a negligent glance at Christine, who seemed to be transfixed before a terrace window, went directly over to the telephone.

"They paid no attention to me whatsoever," he said. "I shudder at what will be the medical examiner's reaction." He jiggled the phone again. "What's the matter with this thing?"

"I think," Christine announced, "that I am going mad."

"You always have been. Why?"

"Stop jiggling that telephone, Stuyvesant. A man just yanked its cord from the connection."

"What man?"

"I haven't the remotest idea. I've written him off as the village idiot."

"Christine, if I ever get you out of this mess I am going to insist on your leaving this unlicensed sanitarium and living in your apartment in town."

Godfrey and Hugo came in, followed by Cordelia, and Hugo said to Christine: "I put him on the couch in your dressing room. Nothing could be done."

"Thank you, Hugo."

"He is covered with a sheet," Godfrey boomed, while Cordelia added sadly, "And there are pennies on his eyes."

Stuyvesant was completely exasperated with all of them.

He said: "I am very much tempted to wash my hands of this whole mess. All of you run counter to every established procedure set up for a death by violence with the serene indifference of people at a tea party—and not *one* of you is even remotely disturbed by the fact that a young woman may be in there freezing to death."

He pointed indignantly toward the quick freezer, and Christine said: "Stuyvesant, Lida can *not* be in there, because the door is locked. Even if she were, she wouldn't freeze. I keep the thermo-stat set at twenty-five above for my furs."

"Freezing," Stuyvesant insisted, "and smothering."

"Nonsense," Hugo said sharply. "There is enough air in that space to maintain life for twenty-four hours."

"Oh it isn't the cold," Cordelia wailed, "it's her being *in* there."

"Cordelia!" Hugo warned in a voice which only made her wail louder and then cover her mouth with her hands as she stared at him in fright.

"Christine," Stuyvesant said, "I demand that that door be smashed open at once."

"Stuyvesant, be calm. I shall settle this nonsense right now. There is a duplicate key in the desk."

Cordelia could not repress a groan, and Godfrey said severely: "Cordelia, Hugo has warned you to control yourself!"

Christine rummaged in a desk drawer and produced a tagged key. Stuyvesant went over and took it from her.

"Let me open the door," he said. "She may be dead. Too."

"Thank you, Stuyvesant."

"You must prepare yourself for a possible further shock."

Stuyvesant, although expecting the worst, was unprepared for the moving heap of fur which hurtled itself at him as he opened the freezer door.

"Help!" Lida shrieked through the sable cape which had slipped over her face in her virile intention to defend herself from the murderer's return. "*Help!*"

Stuyvesant said, "Good God!"

Lida flew at this voice and started pounding its owner on the chest with flapping coat sleeves, screaming: "I won't be murdered too! I won't be!"

"Christine, will you be good enough to control your grand-niece?" Stuyvesant asked.

"Be calm, Miss Belder," Hugo said. "Everything is all right."

"Calm! *Calm?*"

Cordelia ran to her and folded Lida in her arms. "There, there, darling. Everything is all right."

Lida burst into tears against Cordelia's bosom while Stuyvesant, who still stood at the open freezer door, suddenly exploded: "Christine, no—my reason totters—here's another one."

"Another what, Stuyvesant?"

"Corpse, of course."

Lida lifted her head from Cordelia's bosom.

"It's Laura Destin," she said. "She's been murdered." Christine joined Stuyvesant at the freezer.

"Do you remember my warning you that that woman had homicidal tendencies?" he asked her.

"Oh, at least be logical, Stuyvesant. She's the one who is dead. And I'm not." Christine looked inside. "How changed she is. I never would have recognized her. *Is* it Laura? Surely there couldn't be this difference in just a few years—"

"Christine, you yourself change radically every time you re-dye your hair. Who killed her?"

"There's a cut above her lip," Lida said, "where somebody struck her before they smashed her head in. It's the kind of a cut that a ring might make."

"Ring?" Christine repeated sharply.

"Yes, and the lipstick is all smeared."

"Ring—"

"You wouldn't," Hugo suggested, "be thinking of that putrid atrocity which you gave to Alan, would you, Christine?"

"Go and take a look, Hugo—see if there is any cosmetic caught in the prongs." A splitting crash of thunder ripped the air. "Dear, I *wish* it wouldn't do that!"

Hugo went into Christine's suite, and Cordelia said calmly: "It is the end of the storm. The sky will lighten shortly and the sun will come out again."

Stuyvesant pointed indignantly after Hugo. "That man," he said, "will simply create further mischief and mess up evidence which should be kept intact. Christine, I shall take your car and go for the police."

"There are no chains," Godfrey said. "You would go sliding backward down the hill. Telephone—if you insist on being a nuisance."

"I can't telephone. There is no telephone."

"It's right over there, Mr. Swain," Cordelia said helpfully.

"Oh no. Oh, indeed no. You may *think* it is, but it is not."

"Really, Stuyvesant," Christine begged. "Please calm down."

Stuyvesant's blood pressure spilled over and he yelled,

"The village idiot came dancing by and traduced it," as Hugo came back and joined them.

Hugo said to Christine: "There is lipstick stuck in the prongs of Alan's ring." He turned sternly to Cordelia and added: "Do you hear that, Cordelia? The mystery of that woman's death is solved."

"I always thought that Alan did it, Hugo."

"What is more," Godfrey boomed, "his motive is plain. He killed her before she could harm Christine's annuity and stuck her body in the freezer. We need think no more about it."

Lida was beginning to recover sufficiently by now to wonder just what, in this mad scene, was going on. She asked Hugo: "How did Mr. Admont come to let you examine his ring? Wasn't he suspicious? Won't he try to escape?"

"Alan is dead, dear," Christine said. "He was drawing a glass of water in my bathroom. There was a short circuit against the pipes, and the current killed him."

"Oh, Aunt Christine—how terrible!"

"Tragic though it was," Stuyvesant said pompously, "it may all have been for the best. We knew him for a fortune-hunting wastrel, and now we know him to have been a murderer." He paused as above the sound of rain there was a knocking on a terrace door. "Christine, do not attempt to go near that door. As poor Charley's earthly proxy, I feel compelled to see this thing through—in spite of all the warnings of my common sense."

Stuyvesant opened the terrace door, and Sergeant Asher came in.

Handcuffed to Asher was the Dove.

CHAPTER XXIII

Lida took one look at the Dove.

"That's the man!" she cried, not without an amount of venom. "That's the man who strangled me and threw me into the freezer."

"I have been wondering how you got there," Godfrey muttered gloomily.

"Sergeant," Stuyvesant said, "thank goodness you have come."

"Sorry to trouble you again, Mrs. Admont," Asher said, "but this man's car smashed against a rock at the entrance to the Notch. He was semiconscious."

"He *is* semiconscious. He's an idiot. Either local or otherwise. He ripped out my telephone."

Asher took Belle's handbag from under his poncho.

"He had a key with a tag on it stamped Belder Tor, and he had this handbag. The bag is empty, but I figured maybe one of you ladies would recognize it."

"It ought to have three five-hundred-dollar bills in it," Lida said, "and a lipstick that's part of the evidence, although maybe the bit that's ground into the rug will be enough. It belongs to that dead woman, and that man took it before he choked me and threw me into the freezer with her."

Sergeant Asher, who was a step-by-step man, asked: "What dead woman?"

"A Miss Laura Destin, Sergeant," Hugo said patiently. "Mr. Admont murdered her."

"Where's Admont? I'll link him onto this bird."

"You can't. He's dead."

"Suicide?"

"No. Faulty wiring."

Lida's head felt perfectly clear by now. She pointed to the Dove and said: "I don't believe it. I think that man did something to the wires. Aunt Christine, the first moment I saw him he was coming out of your rooms and he said he'd been 'arranging' something and then caught himself and changed it to 'examining' something."

"But why on earth would he, dear? I've never even met him."

Asher looked approvingly at Lida.

"There were electrician's pliers in his brief case and a pair of rubber gloves, to say nothing of a complete chemical outfit and odd bits of wire." Asher gripped the Dove's slender shoulder. "Talk!"

The Dove looked at Asher gently and said: "I do not talk."

"On the contrary," Christine insisted, "he does. Just as he had the infernal impertinence to yank out my telephone, he bewildered me with an abortive philosophical comment on the futility of the best-laid plans of rats and men."

"Rats!" Asher said reflectively.

"The gentleman meant mice, Sergeant," Cordelia explained calmly.

For probably the first time in his life Sergeant Asher used a truly official and commanding voice: "Be still! All of you." He even astonished himself.

"Well, really, Sergeant!"

"Mrs. Admont, a bit of second-story work such as lifting this bag or"—he looked sternly at Cordelia—"some careless absent-mindedness in regard to diamond clips could be handled lightly, but murder cannot be glossed over—not even for a landmark."

Stuyvesant felt this had gone far enough. He swung into his best judicial manner.

"Sergeant Asher, nobody wants to gloss a murder—Mrs. Admont least of all. When you seized upon and emphasized the word 'rats' our minds were in complete accord. You are unquestionably as familiar with the late Mr. Admont's earlier associations with that ex-gangster Joe Inbrun as I am."

"Nobody could help being who could read. They plugged it in all the accounts of the wedding. And I see your point, Mr. Swain. That fortune hunter contacted Inbrun, who sent this lug up to rig a murder trap to bump off his—his—"

"Do be careful, Sergeant," Christine said pleasantly. "Even a landmark does have its feelings."

"But why would poor Alan have fallen into the trap himself?" Cordelia asked.

"Cordelia," Godfrey shouted, "Hugo and I have told you to keep out of this!"

"It is perfectly obvious," Stuyvesant went on happily, "that Mr. Admont did not know what method or device this man would use. And there, Sergeant, is your case."

"There is also, Mr. Swain, this other corpse."

Christine said: "I still cannot believe that that woman was Laura Destin."

Godfrey shouted into the attack: "Suppose, at the greatest stretch of the imagination, she were not? She simply becomes a pitiful creature out of Alan's miserable past who read about the wedding and came here to shake him down—under the threat of exposing him to Christine."

"How little she knew me."

"But she asked for Aunt Christine," Lida said factually, "not Mr. Admont."

Godfrey glared at her balefully.

"Then it was her purpose to sell her knowledge about Alan's past, or else it was revenge of a woman scorned. Do not pester us with these petty details. The broad picture is plain. Alan came upon her and realized her purpose. So he killed her. And now let us say no more about her."

"What proof is there that he killed her?" Asher asked.

"Her lipstick is on his ring from where he struck her across the mouth," Lida said. "And I bet the weapon that gave her the blow on the head was that big flashlight he took upstairs with him last night. I bet there'll be blood on it when you find it, and his finger-prints. Do come and let me show you about the lipstick, Sergeant."

"Bloodthirsty little wretch!" Godfrey muttered.

Lida went to the freezer, and Asher followed, dragging along with him the Dove. Stuyvesant, Christine, and Hugo and Godfrey joined them in crowding before the freezer door.

Cordelia sat placidly in an armchair. She noted vaguely that the Dove, while all the rest were looking into the freezer, had his back to them. It interested Cordelia to watch the gentle, kindly little man while disjointed sentences from the group overlapped each other: "Honestly, Stuyvesant, I do think that Godfrey is right. This is *not* Laura."

"Perhaps he is, Christine, but the structure of the case remains the same. The woman is some impossible adventuress whom that wretch killed. Nothing is of consequence beyond the fact we *know* he killed her."

And Lida was saying simultaneously: "There, Sergeant. You can see where she was first struck on the mouth and then hit on the head. You can compare the lipstick caught in Mr. Admont's ring with that on her mouth, can't you?" And Asher answered: "The B.C.I. boys will handle all that in their laboratory."

How interesting, Cordelia thought while the talk had been going on. She observed the Dove take a ring of keys from his pocket and thoughtfully segregate one of them. Then he unlocked his end of the handcuffs and drifted gently toward a terrace door.

He bowed to Cordelia as he opened it and said: "Good day, madam."

"It is going to be a *lovely* day."

The Dove went, quietly shutting the terrace door, but Cordelia noticed before he did so that the rain had stopped.

Asher said: "As for the Joe Inbrun connection, by the time we get through with this bird—" He lifted the dangling, empty handcuff and realized his prisoner had vanished. "Where is he?"

"He just walked out the terrace door, Sergeant Asher," Cordelia said.

"Oh, he *did*, did he? Mrs. Admont, I'll be back with the boys as soon as I nab that nut again. The case is plainly an open-and-shut one. We will clear up the formalities for you as quickly as we can."

"Thank you, Sergeant Asher. We *are* expecting guests."

Stuyvesant shut his eyes in resignation and murmured: "Charley, it's no use!"

"Which way did he go?" Asher asked Cordelia.

"He went with the rain."

"If you'll excuse me for saying so, Miss Banning, I'd lay off it for a while if I were you."

Asher went out onto the terrace, and the group broke away from the freezer door, which Stuyvesant partially closed.

"Sergeant Asher thinks I'm tight," Cordelia said, "but I'm not. Not the least little bit. I said that the storm was going to clear. The sun will break out any minute now. How good Providence is. How *just!*"

Hugo looked at her sardonically.

"The villains all getting their proper deserts?"

"Yes, Hugo. And the innocent are once more at peace."

Stuyvesant announced decisively: "It is my considered professional opinion that Miss Banning is correct. There will be the formality of a double inquest—on the murderer and his victim. The New York police will handle any Joe Inbrun connection with the case, and this man who obviously is one of his tools. The thing is finished." The sun broke out suddenly and the sky grew bright. An auto horn could be heard blowing a signal in Morse code.

Lida was electrified with joy.

"Barry—oh, listen everybody—that's Barry's signal. He's spelling my name in Morse code." Lida was suddenly stunned. "But this—Oh, Aunt Christine, what will they *think*!"

"My dear Lida," Stuyvesant said acidly, "if you imagine for one moment that your grandaunt is incapable of surmounting a mere matter of murder-plus-corpses, you are simply naïve. I assure you she will surmount not only them but Back Bay."

Christine gave him a fond look.

"Dear Stuyvesant! Run out on the terrace, Lida, and wave to them to use this entrance here."

Lida ran out and stood on the terrace, shading her eyes in the sunshine, looking off toward the driveway for her first glimpse of the car.

Christine at once became the efficient hostess. "Cordelia, do run up and see that the Vanbuskirks' rooms are ready. Do you mind, dear?"

"Of course I will, Christine."

"Just pull up the shades for now. The beds can wait until later."

"And I think while I'm upstairs I'll just pick out some little gift that will be suitable for dear Barry. I *think* there's a pair of cuff links."

Cordelia went up the turret stairs, and Hugo called after her: "Better throw in the keys."

"Godfrey," Christine said, "do be an angel and do something about canapés and lunch."

"Christine, I will surpass even myself. What is that rancid dish so pleasing to Boston stomachs?"

"Scrod."

"There is no scrod. It must be beans."

Godfrey hurried out, and Christine said to Hugo: "The cellaret, Hugo, do you mind? Just wheel it out and restock it, please."

Lida called in from the terrace: "I can see the car!" Hugo started wheeling the cellaret.

"Tea, I suppose, Christine? In magnums?"

"Dear Hugo! What a comfort you are."

"Barry—oh, dear, darling Barry!" Lida cried, and ran off toward the drive.

Christine's efficient eye looked around.

"There is nothing so important when coming to a strange house as a good first impression," she said. "Stuyvesant, shut that freezer door."

Christine walked out onto the terrace and stood there, the gracious hostess, while Stuyvesant, bushed, shut the freezer door.

"Stuyvesant!" Christine called in to him.

"Christine, what now?"

"It's Mr. Vanbuskirk—he's absolutely stunning. He's the *image* of Cordell Hull."

Christine extended her hands in welcome and walked toward the drive.

Stuyvesant, alone in the empty, quiet room, clasped his own hands and lifted his eyes with polite piety to heaven.

"Charley, old man," he said, "I've done my best. But that witch is off again."

ABOUT RUFUS KING

Rufus King (1893–1966) was an American author of Whodunit crime novels. He created four series of detective stories: the first one with Reginald De Puyster, a sophisticated detective similar to Philo Vance; the second one with his more famous character, Lieutenant Valcour; Colin Starr, who appeared in four stories in the *Strand Magazine* during 1940/41; and Detective Bill Duggan, who appeared in three stories in 1956/57. The Bill Duggan stories include his most famous short work, "Malice in Wonderland" (which loaned its title to his 1958 hardcover short story collection).

Modern critics are rediscovering Rufus King's work. Mike Grost, on *Golden Age Detective*, features a long writeup of King, stating: "King had a vivid writing style, with colorful characters, events, and images. He was clearly a born writer."